THE PROMISE

A PASSIONATE TALE OF FAMILY, FRIENDSHIP & LOVE

M.V. KASI

And to ALL my readers and my VIPs!

Thank you for everything.

I love you all!

Contents

Contents

Prologue

"Please stop the car, Vishu!" Bhanu was crying while desperately trying to free her hand from the man's grip.

The pressure of his grip on her wrist only increased further. "No! You are mine, Bhanu. You're coming with me!"

Bhanu let out a sob. The car was going way too fast, but the man didn't seem to care about anything except to get her away from Srirampur.

"Vishu. You are drunk. Please, I beg you. Stop the car!"

The man pulled her arm closer to his face to wipe away his tears using the back of his hand. "How could you do this to us, Bhanu? You know I love you. How could you marry someone else!"

Bhanu's heart broke again for the pain she knew she caused him. "I love him, Vishu," she whispered. "I've always loved him."

"No!" The man shook his head. "You are mine! He doesn't love you. He can never love you the way I do."

Bhanu's lips wobbled because it was the truth. The man she loved didn't love her back. He married her because she had forced him to. They had been married for a month, but he hadn't even touched her or come close to her. He was angry that she had made him betray his friendship to his best friend.

"We'll start a new life, Bhanu. I don't care whether you get an official divorce or not. I don't care if you are already pregnant with that bastard's child, too. I'll be your child's father. It'll be our child. We'll get married and start a family together. I'll keep you happy, Bhanu. I'll give you anything your heart desires. I love you so much."

But my heart desires just him. I only want his love. She wanted to say that but didn't let those words escape her mouth. She knew it would only agitate the man next to her even further.

Before she could plead with him again to let her go, the car came to a sudden halt, jerking her forward.

Relief and fear hit her when she saw the familiar red car. It was her husband.

The next moment, the grip on her wrist was gone when Vishu opened the car door and stepped out.

Bhanu began to panic. Vishu and her husband were of the same height and similar muscular build. They were both well-versed in the art of fighting. While Vishu took pleasure in defeating all of his opponents and thrived on winning the stick-fighting games, her husband was a pacifist who chose not to fight even as a sport. And the fact that both men were close friends since their childhood and shared a rare and unique bond would work against her husband. Her husband would hesitate to raise his hand against the man he loved more than his brother.

"I'm going to kill you!" Vishu shouted at her husband.

"No. Vishu! Stop!" Bhanu got down the car in a panic and ran towards them. She desperately hoped Vishu wouldn't hurt her husband if she begged him not to.

She looked around, and there was no one except for the endless green fields surrounded by the tall coconut and palm trees.

Oh God!

She saw Vishu form a fist and swing his arm towards her husband. She let out a sob, bracing herself to watch her husband get badly hurt, but she was shocked.

The man she loved stopped the oncoming blow using his palm. The next moment, her husband swung his free arm and punched Vishu. He punched him again on his face and then in his stomach. And finally, he shoved Vishu away.

The impact made Vishu stagger and fall on the ground.

Her husband's eyes then fell on her.

Bhanu ran to him and hugged him and cried her heart out. She cried in fear. She cried for the pain she caused the two men. She cried for the love she might never have because of her selfishness.

But instead of pushing her away and giving her a cold, indifferent look, her husband wrapped his arms around her and held her protectively. "Shh. I'm here," he said soothingly. She clung to him and continued to cry.

She heard Vishu groaning at a distance. "Bhanu... Bhanu..." he called out to her repeatedly.

Her husband turned along with her. "Bhanu is my wife," he said in a firm tone. "She doesn't love you. Deal with it. And don't ever show your face to us."

One part of Bhanu's heart that craved this man's love was soothed by those words. But the other part of her heart twisted in agony of the ramifications of him saying those words to Vishu. Bhanu had severed the bond between two men who had promised to remain the closest of friends forever.

Oh God. Please forgive me. I hope this can be set right somehow.

CHAPTER ONE

San Francisco, United States

"Time doesn't wait for anyone. This should've been done yesterday without my presence being required."

Vikram Saaho's firmly uttered words made the silence in the room even more deafening. There were twenty people in the room, seated in comfortable chairs that were made particularly for long hours of conference. And yet, the people fidgeted within ten minutes of the meeting because of the deep, commanding voice and the cutting gaze of the man leading the meeting.

The meeting was taking place inside a high-rise luxury hotel building overlooking the Golden Gate Bridge in the City of San Francisco. It was past dinner time, but half of the people present were used to working around the clock when required.

"Mr. Saaho, I understand your concern. But we are talking about half-a-billion dollars and two thousand employees from my hotel chains."

Vikram Saaho's ruthless gaze intensified on the man seated across the table, making the older man fidget even more. "I perfectly remember all the numbers, Mr. Belmont," Vikram replied. "Considering, I was the one to offer this deal to you." He deliberately used the word 'offer' instead of 'negotiate'. Because just like his grandfather who was the founder of the Saaho Group, Vikram didn't negotiate, he only made offers. And he would be damned if he backed down and be known to cut some slack when reputation was everything in their cutthroat industry.

The older man tried to reason. "The hotel chains have been run by my family for over eighty years. They're one of the most—"

"I already know the history, Mr. Belmont. And we've discussed this before. My legal and financial teams have been working with yours for the past month to alleviate any possible concerns."

The older man fell silent. The Saaho Group was one of the biggest corporations which was well-reputed to acquire failing companies and turn them into profitable businesses in record time. They were also known to offer limited time to accept the deals. And very recently, they had begun to venture out into the hotel industry. So far, the three luxury hotel chains they had acquired in the last three years were thriving quite well.

Taking a deep breath and with slightly trembling hands, Steve Belmont signed the papers. "Done," he said.

"Thank you, Mr. Belmont." Vikram got up and shook the older man's hands. "My team will continue to work with yours during the transition." With those words, he strode out of the meeting room.

Pooja, who was Vikram's executive assistant, joined him inside the elevator. "Vikram, I just received a call. The flight is going to be delayed by a couple of hours due to the unexpected weather conditions. I've already notified the New York office of the delay and to postpone the nine o'clock meeting if required—"

"Not required. I can sleep during the flight." Vikram checked the messages on his phone while the elevator took them down. Most of them were work related, and he promptly replied with his decisions. Only two messages were on his personal account, and they were from his mother.

He clicked on the first message. A picture of a beautiful woman filled the screen. According to the bio-data attached, she was a model. Without pausing for a second, Vikram deleted the entire message. The next message also came in with a picture of another woman. This one was beautiful too, but barely appeared to be out of her teens. She was the daughter of a known industrialist. Vikram deleted this message, too, clearing up his personal inbox.

"Vikram..." Pooja began in a tentative voice. "While you were in the meeting, your mother called me and also sent me messages to let you know that Trisha Seni is in New York right now."

A frown covered Vikram's face. "Trisha Seni?"

"She's a famous model and an aspiring actress who has good family connections and background. She's your mother's good friend's daughter, and your mother mentioned that she already sent Trisha's picture to you. And... Trisha Seni herself has called me to check if you could meet her for dinner tonight. Now that the flight has been delayed..."

Vikram's frown grew.

Pooja hurriedly explained. "I-I know you hate mixing personal things with business. But Mrs. Saaho was insistent. I'm sorry, Vikram."

Vikram knew that although his mother was gentle in nature, she could be pretty assertive in many things, especially when it came to trying to find a perfect match for her elder son. And considering she has been sending him various pictures of eligible women for the past three years, her patience was running low along with her worry.

Even if Vikram had the inclination to marry, at twenty-nine years, he was hardly that old. He worked hard for endless hours, putting in almost a hundred hours a week to further build on the empire his grandfather and father established for the past fifty years. He just didn't think it was time to settle down.

"Let Miss Seni know I won't be able to make it." He gave a quick glance at his watch. There was enough time for him to pick a thoughtful gift for his mother as an apology.

Thirty minutes later, he was getting his mother's gift wrapped while Pooja went to pick a couple of bottles of his father and grandfather's favorite aged single malt whiskey. He was just about to step out of the store when his phone began to ring. It was his mother. Bracing himself for disappointing his mother by not meeting the eligible woman, he answered the call.

"Vikram..." His mother's voice sounded small and tentative. Immediately, Vikram became alert.

"What happened, Mum?"

"It's your grandfather. He's doing fine now, but a few hours ago, he had a stroke while he was in the middle of a meeting."

Vikram was taken aback by the news. Even at nearly seventy-seven years of age, his grandfather was still quite healthy and a force to be reckoned with.

"I know Papa won't like it if I disturb you and Vishu while you're both on business trips. But please, come urgently."

"I'm heading home right away. I'll be there soon, Mum."

"Thank you, son."

As soon as he ended the call with his mother, he called Pooja. "Hi, Vikram, the pilot just called and said we can take off anytime now."

"Call him back," Vikram instructed. "Tell him we're flying home to London."

***

3

Paris, France

Vishal Saaho stirred and groaned softly to the sound of a ringing phone. It was still dark outside. Only a couple of hours must have passed since he fell asleep around three in the morning.

He groaned once again, recognizing the ring tone and knowing quite well that even though it was an ungodly hour, the person wouldn't stop calling until the phone was answered.

Shifting to his side and gently prying away the two sets of feminine arms wrapped around his bare torso, Vishal reached for his phone.

"Where are you, Vishal?" Vikram's voice asked.

"Still in Paris." Vishal's gaze fell on the view outside the Eifel Tower surrounded by a heavy mist.

"You already closed the deal last evening. Why are you still there?"

Vishal grinned recalling the reason. "The former chairman's daughter wanted me to stay after we closed the deal. I agreed. Just to ensure that there are no hard feelings remaining after the acquisition. Anyway, I'm flying to Sydney in a few hours."

"Not Sydney. Go home. I'm flying home, too."

Vishal's grin disappeared and a frown took over. "What happened?"

"Grandfather's fine now. But he had a stroke a couple of hours back."

"Grandfather?" The tough old taskmaster was healthy as a horse and even jogged three kilometers each morning. The head of the Saaho Group still put the fear of God in everyone who worked for him. If anything, the people around him should have heart attacks and strokes. How the hell did he have a stroke?

"He's seventy-seven, Vishal. These things are bound to happen." Vikram knew how attached and how much Vishal loved their grandfather. "Get on the next flight and go home. Mum and Dad need us now."

"I'll leave right away." Vishal ended the call and then dialed the number of his personal assistant. As soon as the phone was answered, he instructed his assistant to make the necessary arrangements.

Vishal stepped down from the bed. Not bothering to search for his discarded clothes among the scattered clothes around the room, he headed to the bathroom.

A quick, cold shower later, he felt awake despite two hours of sleep. Just when he had put on a fresh pair of clothes and was zipping his suitcase, his attention fell on the stirring on the bed. One of the two women sat up and looked at him.

"Vishal? You're leaving already?"

"Yeah. Got an emergency call from home," he told her. "You and your girlfriend are more than welcome to stay longer in the hotel suite. Order breakfast, lunch or even drinks. I'll tell the management to keep the tab open on my account."

He smiled at the slightly smitten and bemused look on the woman's beautiful face. Considering that her preferences had always leaned towards other females, he could understand her shock when she along with her long-time girlfriend decided to spend the night with him in his bed.

"Take care, sweetheart," he told her. "And all the best for your wedding."

He wheeled his suitcase out of the hotel suite.

Tanuj, Vishal's personal assistant, was already waiting downstairs. Sliding into the sleek, black limousine that would take them to the airport, Vishal gave out more instructions to Tanuj before calling his mother and assuring her everything would be fine.

CHAPTER TWO

London, United Kingdom

"He was talking during the meeting when his breathing started to become uneven. A few minutes later, he was clutching his head. I rushed him to the hospital right away."

Rajesh Saaho was telling Vikram what had happened with his father. They were all at the Saaho house. Vishal had arrived a few hours earlier and accompanied his parents while they shifted the still unconscious Saaho patriarch from the hospital to their home.

"Grandfather is going to be okay, Dad," Vishal assured once again. "The old coot is most likely going to outlive us all."

Vinita Saaho smiled, but there was worry in her eyes. "I know he'll be fine this time, Vishu. But I'm worried that the stroke wasn't a random one. For the past few months, your dad and I have noticed that Papa seemed distracted."

"Distracted, how?" Vikram asked while waving away the offer for tea that was being served by their housekeeper.

While Vishwanath Saaho was being monitored by a team of nurses in his suite, the rest of the family were all seated in their large living room.

"Sometimes, Papa just sits quietly and contemplates," Vinita Saaho continued. "He was even going through a few old family albums. We thought he must be missing Mamma."

"He must be," Vishal added. Most of his life, Vishwanath Saaho had been busy building his empire rather than dedicating time to his wife or family. It was only during the last three years before his wife had passed away due to a terminal illness that Vishwanath Saaho spent quality time with her.

"Papa has been making enquiries and monitoring someone who lives in Srirampur," Rajesh Saaho added with a frown.

"Srirampur?" Vikram frowned similarly.

"It's a village in India," said Vinita. "Although Papa has never mentioned it to us, I have a feeling he's from that place or knows someone there."

"But Grandfather loathes India," said Vishal. "He doesn't even want us to do any business in the entire country even though it has great potential."

Vikram and Vishal had never visited India. Their other set of grandparents and extended family from their mother's side were sent tickets to fly to London whenever they wanted to meet their daughter and her family. Apart from making charitable donations, the Saaho Group didn't make any investments in India.

"Unless Papa wakes up, we can't speculate," Rajesh Saaho stated.

Which everyone agreed to.

Later that night, after checking on her father-in-law who was still hadn't gained consciousness, Vinita knocked on the door of her older son's suite.

It was quite rare to have both Vikram and Vishal home at the same time for this long. Both her sons were always on the go, flying around the world or staying in their penthouses in the city which were closer to their offices. Only when it was her birthday or some rare occasion, her sons made it a point to stay at their childhood home for a day or so to spend some quality time with her.

Vikram answered the door, and Vinita could hear the background noise of an ongoing meeting. "Mum? Everything okay?" he asked.

"Yes. Papa is fine, too. He's still sleeping." She went in and sat on a small antique sofa that had been in this room since Vikram's childhood.

"Did you get a chance to meet Trisha Seni?" she asked.

Vikram's eyebrows drew into a frown. "Who?"

Vinita was exasperated and worried about her eldest born. "I sent you Trisha's picture and even let Pooja know that Trisha will be in New York at the time of your visit."

"I didn't find any time."

Vinita sighed. "Vikram, Trisha is a nice girl. Her mother is a good friend of mine. I feel—"

"Mum," Vikram gently interrupted her. "Let it go. I told you I'd find a woman to marry when the timing is right."

Vinita had heard the same statement repeated several times over the past three years. "And when will the right time come, son?" she asked. "I know you want to conquer the world. But you need to slow down a little, or you'll burn out after becoming too detached from everything."

She was worried how similar Vikram was to Vishwanath Saaho whose life revolved around his work and never his family. Vinita recalled how lonely her mother-in-law had felt, which led to a close friendship and bond between Vinita and her. And only when Vinita's mother-in-law was diagnosed with a rare lung disease did Vishwanath Saaho realize how much his wife meant to him. He only spent the last few years exclusively with her until she passed away in her sleep.

Since then, it led him to develop a slightly closer bond with his son and the rest of his family. But Vinita didn't want the death of a loved one to make Vikram realize that life was short, and that love and family were priorities along with work.

"I'll be fine, Mum. Here, this is for you." He handed her a beautiful hand-knitted scarf.

Vinita thanked him before letting him continue with his meetings. She stepped out and went towards Vishal's room.

Just as she was about to knock on the door, she heard voices. A sultry and seemingly familiar voice of a woman could be heard.

"Come on, Vishal. Your reputation and wild exploits are well known," the woman said.

"I don't exploit," Vishal's tone was cold and flat. "And if you really researched about me as you claim, you should've already known that I don't get involved with women my family or I employ. And I find it in extremely bad taste that we're even having this conversation in my parents' house."

"But I went through so much to be appointed as one of Mr. Saaho's personal nurses—"

"Then leave before I consider firing you."

There was silence. Vinita stepped into a small nook away from the door. Soon, the door opened and she saw one of the nurses exiting with a disappointed look on her face.

Waiting for half-a-minute longer, Vinita went inside her son's room.

Vishal turned towards the door with a frown. But as soon as he saw her, a ready dimpled smile was followed by a bear hug. "Mum!"

"Busy?" she asked with a similar matching dimpled smile.

Something flashed in his eyes, but he continued to smile. "Not really. One of Grandfather's nurses just came in to let me know he's doing well."

Vinita felt proud of her younger son for not outing the nurse. Although he had a reputation for playing as hard as he worked and leading a wild, fast life... underneath it all, he was always considerate and followed his code of honor to the T.

She chatted with Vishal for some time.

"All right, son. You must be tired. I'll talk to you tomorrow," she said.

"Goodnight, Mum."

Kissing Vishal goodnight, she headed back to her suite.

As soon as Vinita stepped into her bedroom, her eyes fell on her husband who was leaning back against their headboard and reading a book while wearing his reading glasses.

With his strong, masculine features and the prominent grays near his temples, even in his fifties, Rajesh Saaho was quite dashing and handsome. She recalled how thrilled and excited she had been thirty years ago that the well-known Saahos had chosen her to be their daughter-in-law even though she came from a middle-class family. She was smitten and blown away by the young, dynamic Rajesh Saaho.

But it wasn't always a smooth ride. Because very early on she realized that her husband was a workaholic and didn't have much time to spare for her. It took her a lot of effort and heartache and even a brief separation to make Rajesh realize that family was a priority too. Of course, her mother-in-law had supported her every step of the way. Rajesh Saaho was now a proper family man.

Rajesh looked up from the book. "Done talking to your sons?" he asked with a smile.

"Yes," she replied.

He put the book aside along with his spectacles. He didn't bring work or technology into their bedroom. It was one of the many rules they mutually agreed upon.

She lay on the bed and sighed. "Vikram didn't meet or even bother to speak to Trisha."

Rajesh wrapped an arm around her waist and pulled her closer until they were in the position they usually slept in. "He's only twenty-nine, sweetheart. Let's give him some more time."

"Well, you got married when you were twenty-three, and Vikram was born when you were twenty-four!"

There was laughter. "What can I say? I was blown away by the beautiful picture my mother waved in front of me. And even more so when I met you."

Vinita smiled. It never got old how many ever times they spoke on the topic of how they had met and married.

"Vishu is twenty-six," said Rajesh. "Why don't you insist on pursuing Vishu's marriage like you do for Vikram's?"

Vinita laughed. "Because in Vishu's case, we'll probably have grandchildren regardless of him being married or not. But I'll be happier if we were to have a daughter-in-law first before being presented with a grandchild."

Rajesh laughed. "Don't worry, my love. It's only a matter of time. Both our sons will soon marry and we'll have enough grandchildren to pamper. And I can bet that Papa will be there to see his great-grandchildren, too."

Vinita sighed in contentment imagining that scenario. "I really hope so."

***

The next morning, the Saaho family members woke up to the news that Vishwanath Saaho had regained consciousness.

CHAPTER THREE

Vishwanath Saaho opened his eyes to the familiar room which he had been living in for the past fifty years.

However, the tubes and the beeping machines along with a group of uniformed nurses was an unfamiliar sight. He pulled off the mask from his face and was about to demand that the machines be cleared from his room, but his voice didn't seem to work.

He was just about to call for a nurse when his eyes fell on his family who had just joined him inside the room. Vinita, his dear daughter-in-law who was more like a daughter to him, had a worried look on her face. As usual, nothing could be read from Rajesh and Vikram's expression. And Vishal's ever-present smirk or smile was absent as well. What the hell had happened?

"I hope you're feeling better now, Papa," Vinita said in a gentle tone.

Vishwanath nodded.

"Do you recall having a stroke during the meeting?" Rajesh asked.

Vishwanath just shrugged.

Rajesh and Vinita didn't say it aloud, but Vishwanath was reminded of all the times in recent years when they had both demanded that he take it slow when it came to his workload. But years of habit were hard to let go.

Even though Vishwanath appeared to be cool and accepting on the outside, he felt a bit shaken on the inside with the news of his stroke. Not because of death which he knew at his age was inevitable. It was because his stroke meant there wasn't as much time as he thought he would have. And there was a good possibility that he could die without making amends.

Some of his panic must have conveyed on his face.

"I would like everyone to step out for a while and give my family some privacy." At Vikram's order, the group of nurses stepped out.

Vishwanath slowly tried to sit up. Immediately, Vikram and Vishal helped him and placed a few pillows at his back until he was seated comfortably on the bed. Vishwanath's eyes fell on both his grandsons. Pride filled him as always. Although Vikram and Vishal were very different in temperament, they were both known in the business world for achieving success in whatever tasks they took upon themselves. Vikram was more like him, firm and demanding, while Vishal was a charismatic charmer who got things done through his oratory skills.

Slowly an idea took root in Vishwanath's mind. And unlike all the other times in the last three years, he felt a twinge of hope. He directed his eyes towards his office desk. Vinita understood immediately and brought him the book along with a pen.

With badly shaking hands, he began to write on the paper.

Vikram and Vishal. I need your help.

CHAPTER FOUR

"You think you know everything about a person because you've known and loved them for so long... and yet... someday you realize there's so much more that you don't know about them."

Vinita Saaho's statement resonated with her husband and sons.

After spending the last couple of hours with Vishwanath Saaho, they all had more questions than answers. Vishwanath Saaho had asked Vikram and Vishal to help him fulfill a promise. Along with it, he had written the name of a man who lives in a village called Srirampur. And the most shocking part was when he had also written that the man was his childhood friend who now hated Vishwanath Sahoo.

"Are you both sure you want to go?" Rajesh asked his sons. "Maybe I should just go and speak to that person instead."

"No, Dad," said Vikram. "Grandfather wants Vishal and me to do it, and we'll do this for him."

"But if that man hates your grandfather, how will you both convince him to see your grandfather?"

"We don't know that yet, but we are determined to do this for Grandfather."

Rajesh felt uncertain, but he nodded. "I'll manage things over here while you both are gone," he said. His eyes fell on his smiling wife. "What?"

"I'm excited that Vikram and Vishal will be going to India for the first time and that too to a village." She looked at her sons. "You know you both will have to take a break from work."

"We're quite aware, Mum," Vikram said drily. "But however remote the village is, our satellite phones and internet should still be able to work."

Vinita shook her head before looking at her younger son. Her smile widened. "And you, my love, however brief the stay is, I'm hoping that you see and appreciate what a laid-back life looks like, unlike your too-fast one."

Vishal was amused. "Our visit would probably only last a couple of days or a week maximum, Mum," he said confidently. "How hard can it be to impress someone and then convince them to meet an old childhood friend?"

***

"It's not going to be easy at all. Suryaprakash Gulati is known for holding long grudges as much as he's known for his charitable ways."

Vikram's assistant, Pooja, was updating the Saaho family with the information the investigative team had gathered so far in the last two days. "Suryaprakash Gulati is extremely involved in the development schemes of his village. But he still hasn't touched or used any money that came from outside India. He hates what he terms as NRI money."

"Does it have anything to do with Vishwanath Saaho?" Vinita asked.

"I'm not sure, madam. We weren't able to gather that piece of information yet."

"We'll probably have to wait until Papa can speak," Rajesh Saaho added. "Until then, we need to go with whatever we have."

Vikram picked up the file on Suryaprakash. "What do you mean by charitable ways?" he asked Pooja.

"Suryaprakash Gulati has donated more than fifty percent of his ancestral lands and money to the villagers and also used it for various development schemes. Apparently, if you impress him enough, he would be willing to help or do anything you want. People line up to work for him, so that they can get a piece of land or a chunk of money or ask for huge favors when they please him enough."

There was silence.

"Pooja, excuse us for a while," said Vikram.

As soon as Pooja left, Vinita was the one to speak. "I know what you are all thinking. I'm not sure if we should take advantage of a generous, unsuspecting man."

"At the end of it, they'll be helping two good friends get together," Rajesh Saaho tried to reason with his wife.

"Maybe so. But it's definitely a grey area."

"What other choice do we have, Mum?" Vishal asked. "If the man is the type to hold grudges, he isn't going to relent if we go and talk to him as Vishwanath Saaho's grandsons."

Vikram was silent. He was reading the rest of the information on the file.

"If not as Vishwanath Saaho's grandsons, how else are you both planning to impress Suryaprakash?"

Vikram was the one to answer his mother. "As his accountant and driver."

CHAPTER FIVE

A week later, a private jet with the words *Saaho Group* blazed across it landed in India.

An entourage of assistants and bodyguards accompanied Vikram and Vishal as they checked into a penthouse hotel suite. Nobody had the time to relax. The questions along with the preparations continued.

"And what about the rest of the people working in Suryaprakash's household?" Vishal asked looking at the file.

"There are two other people in Mr. Suryaprakash's employ," Tanuj replied. "But we have only made contact with the accountant and driver. It seemed too risky to make contact with the other two as they have been working for him for way too long."

"Good," said Vikram. "We can't afford to change our plan at the last moment. Just ensure that the driver and the accountant remain silent and bound to the contract they signed. Don't skimp or bargain with whatever amount of money they had demanded."

Tanuj nodded. Meantime, Pooja pulled out another file and placed it on the table. "This one is about Mr. Suryaprakash's family. His granddaughters—"

"I already told you before not to bother with his family," Vikram interrupted. "Just focus on the man we are to impress."

Pooja nodded and put the file aside.

Vishal looked at Tanuj. "How much longer for the rest of the preparations?"

"Your new clothes and required accessories will be delivered to the suite this evening. And the driver's licenses and IDs will be arriving tomorrow."

It had been less than twenty hours since they landed in India. Considering the progress so far, Vikram and Vishal should have been impressed. But they weren't. They were both impatient to get to the actual person and begin their charade.

"There's one more important thing," Pooja said tentatively. "We need to brief you both on the customs and traditions of the villages. We hired a consultant for that job."

"Where is he?"

"He's in the lobby of the hotel, waiting to be summoned if you want him."

Vikram looked at Vishal who shrugged. "We might as well know to make things a bit simpler during our stay."

***

If only it were that simple. The consulting was brutal. The consultant went through every possible custom, some of which Vikram and Vishal already knew as their mother was particular of those traditions.

"What do you mean by orthodox? We consider ourselves to be somewhat orthodox, too," Vishal interrupted when the man continued on yet another long lecture.

"No offense, sir," the consultant replied. "By orthodox, I mean that if you talk or show interest in a girl, you are expected to marry her."

Vishal looked horrified. "If you just talk?"

"Well... maybe times have changed, but not by much. Talking is fine. But any sort of romantic touching is a strict intent to marry."

Much later, when the consultant finally left, Vishal shook his head in disbelief. "Well, it's a good thing neither of us plans to even see, let alone touch anyone in the romantic sense during our charade."

Looking at the horrified look on Vishal's face, "Are you sure?" Vikram asked with a touch of amusement.

"Most definitely! Can you imagine me ever having to marry at my age? And that too to a naive woman who is from a village?"

"Based on your attention span when it comes to the women you date, no."

Vishal chuckled. He gazed out of the large window that overlooked the bustling city.

"Would you like me to arrange for dinner at an exclusive restaurant in the city?" Tanuj asked.

"No," Vikram replied. "There is a lot of pending handover before I go off the grid."

It was a Saturday and most parts of the world weren't working. But Tanuj expected that of the older Saaho brother. He then looked at his employer and got the answer he predicted.

Vishal Saaho smiled. "Make arrangements at the best nightclub this city has to offer."

CHAPTER SIX

The next day, the deafening sound of the rotating blades of a helicopter filled the air as it landed in the middle of bright green fields. The chopper waited while Vikram and Vishal continued to give instructions to their assistants on what was needed to be done during their absence.

A few minutes later, Pooja interrupted. "Vikram," she said. "It's time for the bus to arrive. Here are the tickets." She handed them over.

Tanuj handed a small folder to Vishal. "Your new driver's licenses," he said.

Soon, the brothers got out of the chopper with their carry bags and walked towards the other side of the road.

Pooja and Tanuj let out a deep sigh of relief. It had been quite a hectic week. Working as Vikram and Vishal's personal assistants had never been a cakewalk. They had to put in equally long and hard hours as their employers. And added to that was the chaos from the last few days to prepare their employers for a perfect charade.

Tanuj let out another sigh. "Do you think people would believe that they are both down-on-their-luck lower-middle-class men seeking employment? Rather than billionaires who would one day inherit a company whose GDP is a little more than that of a small country?"

Pooja stared at the two men heading towards the place where a bus would soon arrive. "We both worked our asses off to prepare them for that look. So, I really hope people believe them." Even as she said that, she knew that she personally wouldn't believe that they were anything but themselves.

Even with their modest clothing, the way the Saaho brothers carried themselves was a dead giveaway. They looked like people who were used to commanding rather than taking orders.

***

A red colored bus arrived within five minutes of waiting.

"Where to?" the ticket collector asked.

"Srirampur." Vikram got on the bus and handed the tickets. He chose the front-row seat and Vishal sat next to him.

"You know it's odd," the ticket collector said while handing back their tickets. "Usually this bus is brimming with people seated inside and also with people seated on the top of the bus. Earlier this morning when I checked, the tickets were sold out as usual, and I thought we would have full capacity."

Vishal shrugged. "Strange indeed." He was the one to order Tanuj to buy out all the tickets to the bus which would take them to the village.

"So whom are you meeting in Srirampur?" the ticket collector asked.

"No one in particular," Vishal replied. "We heard so many good things about the village that we decided to find jobs there. Maybe we'll meet with the head of the village."

The ticket collector nodded his head enthusiastically. "Yes. Mr. Suryaprakash will definitely help you. He helps everyone in need. Although..." His eyes swept over Vishal and Vikram. "Although I'm not sure what men like you would do in a village."

"Men like us?" Vikram asked with a raised eyebrow.

"You both seem like you're from the city and accustomed to the city life. And you seem to be doing well, too."

Vishal frowned. He and his brother had specifically worn cheap, modest clothes and even packed accordingly.

"Maybe it's just the way you're dressed, I suppose," the ticket collector added.

"We decided to dress... in our best clothes when we're looking for jobs."

The other man didn't look convinced by Vishal's explanation, but he nodded. "Mr. Suryaprakash always gives opportunity to people in need. He will definitely hire you both."

That little piece of information was part of the investigative report they'd received of Suryaprakash Gulati.

The man continued to chat, giving them pretty much the same information they'd learned in the last few days. Finally, their stop arrived. "It's a thirty-minute walk from here."

Thanking the man and the driver, Vikram and Vishal got down from the bus. As soon as the bus drove away, Vishal pulled his tucked shirt from the waistband and crumpled it slightly. And then, he messed up his hair before finger-combing it randomly.

He reached a hand to mess up his brother's hair. Vikram moved away with a frown.

"Come on, bro. We need to look the part," Vishal insisted. "That means you don't show up with neatly styled hair with an expensive gel in it. And now that I think about it, maybe you should lose a button or two from your shirt."

Vikram continued to frown. "I'm fine," he said. His eyes fell on a tap at a distance where large earthen pots of drinking water were also kept to the side. He walked to the place and turned the tap on and kept his head under it. Then standing back up, he finger-combed his hair. But he left his shirt neatly tucked in. He drew a line when it came to his clothes. Cheap was fine, but shabby definitely was not.

Vishal laughed. "Let's go, big brother. Let's get this charade over with."

CHAPTER SEVEN

The place where Vikram and Vishal were dropped off was just outside the village entrance. They were distracted during the helicopter ride and also during most of their bus ride. But now, they had the time to take in their surroundings.

Green fields surrounded one side of the road. The other side was the village entrance. The roads were clean but quite narrow. Some of the ones that went into the inner streets seemed to be just mud roads.

As they walked further inside, they took in more details.

There were giggling and laughing women going about their chores. They were all dressed in traditional attire. Even the men wore traditional attire. The kids played with each other or with wooden toys rather than videogames or remote-controlled cars.

Everyone noticed them, but only a man came forward. "Who are you?"

"Vikram and Vishal Reddy," Vikram replied. "We have come to seek jobs and would like to meet the village head."

The village man frowned at the soft yet demanding tone, but he didn't dare argue seeing the look on Vikram's face.

Vishal spoke to the man before other people decided to intervene. "What my brother means is that we would really appreciate it if you can help us find the house of Mr. Suryaprakash."

Immediately, the man's expression changed. "Oh. You're here for Mr. Suryaprakash. Why didn't you say so in the beginning? Come. I'll take you there."

The man chatted with them as they walked. He asked the same questions as the ticket collector had asked, and he received the same answers as what Vikram and Vishal had practiced. Soon, they arrived in front of a sprawling, old-fashioned two-story house that was beginning to show its age. "This is Mr. Suryaprakash's house," said the man.

Thanking him, Vikram and Vishal promised to meet up with the man soon.

Shrieks and yelling could be heard from inside. Vikram pushed open a large gate when a child came hurtling towards them from within the house. The small boy was being chased by a woman.

"Come back here!" she shouted.

"No! I know you'll hurt me!" the boy shouted.

The woman's eyes fell on Vikram. "Catch him!" she ordered. "Don't let him escape the gate!"

Vishal was highly amused by the look on his brother's face at the order. The woman was very pretty, and she was wearing similar traditional attire as the other women from the village had worn. Although, the material of the cloth seemed more expensive than what the other women wore. And on top of her dress, she was wearing a long, white coat.

Another man exited the house and followed behind the woman holding a box.

"Well?" the woman looked at Vikram and demanded. "Move! Time doesn't wait for anyone," she said.

That statement shocked Vishal, and he was sure his brother was taken aback too. It was a statement Vikram often used because their grandfather had taught them that while they were growing up.

Since his brother seemed too bemused to react, Vishal caught hold of the child. The boy squirmed in his arms. "Let me go! She's going to give me an injection!"

The pretty woman closed the distance between them. "Of course! Did I not warn you not to tease the puppies? Now that you have been bitten, you have to take the shots, or you'll fall very sick since they are not yet vaccinated."

"No! No!" the child in Vishal's arms wailed.

The woman turned to Vikram. "Here. Hold this," she said, handing a medium-sized medical kit.

Vikram held it while she drew out a syringe. The man who had come behind her handed her gloves. The woman's entire concentration was on preparing the shot she was about to give the child.

Vishal wondered whether she was one of the granddaughters of Suryaprakash. All he knew was there were two granddaughters, and one of them was a school girl and nothing much. Damn, now he regretted that unlike his brother, at least he should have picked up that file about them and read through it. Now, he would have to wait until he had enough privacy to call and get the updates from Tanuj or Pooja.

Vishal's thoughts were interrupted when the kid in his arms began shrieking. Vishal was having a devil of a time trying to keep the child still without putting too much pressure on him.

"Stop it." At Vikram's command, the little kid's eye grew larger, and he immediately stopped shrieking.

"All done," the woman told the child with a smile. "See. I told you, it would hardly hurt. You wasted so much time making us run around the house. Now go inside and ask for a sweet from the kitchen."

When the kid squirmed again, Vishal let him go. The kid immediately broke into a run and went towards the house.

Wiping her hands with a wet tissue that smelled of antiseptic, the woman asked, "Who are you both again?"

"We're here to meet Mr. Suryaprakash," Vishal replied.

"Grandpa is inside. But why are you here to meet him?" she asked.

"We're looking for jobs," Vikram replied.

She looked at them and a confused look passed on her face. "Jobs in my village?"

"Yes."

"As what?" she asked curiously. The woman took in their appearances closely this time. Vishal noticed that her eyes lingered a few moments longer on Vikram, who with his neatly tucked shirt, hardly looked like he would plough the fields or do any sort of manual labor.

"We don't know that yet," Vikram replied. "Maybe your grandfather can suggest something."

"Huh, interesting," she remarked. "Come inside." She looked at the other man who was holding a small medical kit. "Go back to the clinic. If there's a patient, send for me. I'll be inside the house."

Vikram and Vishal followed her as she went into the sprawling home.

"This is the visitor's room. Be seated here. I'll go find my grandfather." She disappeared into another room. "Grandpa, someone is here to see you!" she announced.

She then came back to the visitor's room and took a chair opposite to them. "You both don't seem like you belong to any of the surrounding villages," she said. Then her eyes lingered again on Vikram with a thoughtful look. "Or for that matter, to any village."

"We're not from a village," Vikram replied.

The woman's eyes sparkled with curiosity again. "Then why are you looking for jobs in my village?"

Before either of the brothers could reply, they heard the voice of another man—an older man.

"Who is it, Geeta?" the man asked.

A minute later, a man who was similar in age to Vishwanath Saaho came into view. Just like in his pictures, standing tall and straight, even at his age and with a mustache twirled at the ends, Suryaprakash Gulati cut an impressive figure.

Vikram and Vishal stood up to greet the older man. The man nodded regally.

"Grandpa, these two men wanted to meet you to see if you can help them look for jobs in our village."

Before the older man could speak, Vishal broke into the rehearsed explanation. "Sir, I'm Vishal and this is my brother, Vikram. We've come from the city," he said. "My brother and I lost our jobs recently. And since we hated leading the monotonous and busy lives in the city, we both decided to settle in a village. We've heard so much about Srirampur and how people living here lead a content and satisfying life, we decided to settle here. We would like to request you to please help us find jobs and accept us into your community."

Suryaprakash listened quietly. After Vishal was done talking, the older man didn't ask him any questions or seem remotely suspicious. In fact, the older man looked proud.

"I know that the city life can be quite monotonous, sometimes with disconnect between people living together, too. You both made the right decision to settle in one of the villages, which is where the true soul of India exists. And Srirampur is by far one of the best places to settle down in life." He assessed them closely. "Are you here with your families?"

"No, sir," Vishal replied. "Our parents work in the city. And my brother and I are not married yet."

"Hmm... So what jobs did you both have before?"

"I was working as a cashier in a bank," Vikram replied. "And my brother was working as a driver for a company."

"I see." Suryaprakash appeared thoughtful. "Well, we do have a bank in the neighboring village, but the staff is already full." He looked at Vikram. "Would you be opposed to working for me as a full-time accountant instead?"

"I'd be happy to take it up, sir."

Suryaprakash looked at Vishal. "You're quite lucky because our driver left the village a week ago, and I was on the lookout for a driver."

"I sure am lucky, sir," Vishal said with a smile.

The older man nodded. "My accountant and my driver used to stay with us. Do you both mind living in this house?"

"We'd be happy to stay, sir."

"That's good. We have two rooms, one inside the house and the other outside, behind the barn. Lakshmi will show you both your rooms and also help you with anything you want."

As though on cue, a grey-haired woman who appeared to be in her sixties came forward. She was watching Vikram and Vishal intently.

"Follow me," she finally said.

CHAPTER EIGHT

"Grandpa. You think they're trustworthy?" Sangeeta asked as soon as Lakshmi led the new employees away to show them their rooms.

"They want to rebuild their lives here, Geeta. Everyone deserves a second chance."

Sangeeta smiled. "True." But soon, her expression became stern. "I noticed that you haven't taken the medicines I kept on your table."

"I will now, Doctor Madam."

Sangeeta laughed. "All right, Grandpa. I'll head back to the clinic. I'll see you later."

As Sangeeta headed back to the clinic, her thoughts ran to the two newcomers. They didn't seem like they were down-on-their-luck men. The way they both carried themselves and the way they dressed seemed like they were well-to-do people.

Maybe it was the case of judging people the opposite way. Just because they were well put together didn't necessarily mean they were not going through hard times. And besides, why would anyone go through the trouble of coming this far to Srirampur and finding jobs at her grandfather's house. It wasn't like her grandfather was rich or had many valuables at home.

The only things that were valuable were the simple gold jewellery that Sangeeta's late grandmother had owned and passed them to Sangeeta and her sister.

Sangeeta shook her head. She was reading too much into the newcomers' entry into her home.

"Doctor Madam! Quick!" Sangeeta's assistant, Kailash, said urgently. "Badhra cut his hand while working in the fields. He's in the clinic right now."

Sangeeta didn't waste any more time thinking of the newcomers and slipped into her professional mode. "Let's go." She began to instruct what needed to be done as soon as they reached the clinic.

***

"The room isn't that big," the old woman named Lakshmi stated. "But it's the only room that we have available. Two other rooms that are slightly bigger are occupied by the cook and me."

Vikram glanced briefly at the tiny yet clean room. "This will do." Or rather he had no choice but to accept it. He was about to reach for his wallet to tip the woman and stopped at the last moment. Some habits die hard.

Lakshmi looked at Vishal. "Your room is at the back of the house, next to the barn."

"I'll find it by myself. I'll help my brother settle in first."

The older woman nodded. "Lunch has already been served, but you can go into the kitchen at any time during the day and ask for a meal. I'll come back later to show you the rest of the house."

As soon as she left the room, Vishal crashed on the bed with a sigh.

"Help me settle? Settle with what?" Vikram asked with a raised brow.

Vishal smirked. "Don't be a snob, bro. I know this place doesn't meet with your high standards, especially since you're used to acquiring and staying in the world's most luxurious hotels."

"So are you," Vikram added drily.

"Nevertheless," Vishal continued with a grin. "I can help you spread the high thread count bed sheet that Mum packed for you."

"Thanks. But I'm perfectly capable of spreading my own bed sheets... I think."

Vishal burst out laughing.

Vikram shook his head with a smile. He then put his bag on the corner of the bed and pulled out his cell phone. "I'm going to send a message to Mum that we have arrived. And I'll have to catch up with my email and some pending instructions. I'll come by later to your room."

"All right. Even if our company is currently up in flames because of your absence, keep your voice low. I'm pretty sure an accountant constantly barking orders on the phone will raise red flags." Vishal picked up his bag. "Catch you later, bro."

Whistling softly, Vishal went out of the house and towards the back of the house where he had seen a barn-like structure. He saw a few men and women working outside the house. It was a warm day and most of the men were working shirtless. Beads of sweat ran down Vishal's temple and on his back. He wanted to change out of his clothes and take a long, cold shower.

With a sigh, hoping his stay wouldn't demand he remain long in this hot weather, he continued to the barn.

The barn had no animals in it. Just a few puppies playing inside. There were several bags possibly with grain inside stored against the wall. The rest of the space was filled with a few heaps of hay. The pleasant smell of fresh hay was quite nice. He had seen a couple of cows tied on the other side of the house, and he had even heard the sound of chickens.

The last time he had been to a farm was during one of the family vacations. At that time, he was ten, so he was thrilled seeing and spending time with the farm animals. He hoped that his stay here, sans the fast life he was accustomed to, would be equally interesting.

He went towards the back of the barn where a rickety door was present. Luckily it was unlocked. He threw the bag over his shoulder and pushed the door open and stepped in.

He saw a young boy removing his t-shirt. Vishal put his bag to a corner and looked around the room. It was small and slightly dusty with a single cot with a thin mattress on top.

Vishal sighed. At least there was good ventilation.

His attention fell on the boy who was grunting softly while still desperately trying to wiggle out of a t-shirt. With a frown, Vishal went to help. He wanted the kid out so he could relax in peace and also make the phone calls to catch up with his pending work.

Holding the ends of the boy's t-shirt, Vishal tugged it hard. There was a loud rip, and the boy was freed.

Vishal stared at the boy who was actually a girl.

His eyes met with a pair of dark brown eyes on a pretty face. Those eyes were at first blank, then shocked, and then finally furious.

"How dare you!" She hissed before slapping him hard. For a small woman who barely came up to his shoulders, she packed quite a punch. She didn't stop with the slap, she came at him with her fingers bent like claws.

"Whoa, whoa. Easy there, woman." He caught her hand as she tried to scratch his eyes out.

"I'm going to kill you, you dirty bastard!"

"Hey..." He tried protesting while trying to control the furious woman without using undue force. But the woman's anger gave her enough strength.

"Let me go, you sick asshole. You..." She continued using words that would put a swearing sailor to shame. And most of the words he had no clue what they meant, but he could get the underlying gist.

"All right, enough. I thought you were a—" He broke off and hissed due to pain. The woman had bitten him.

"Stop it!" he ordered. But the woman was too enraged to listen to reason.

When she bent down to bite him again, he had no choice but to turn her around and wrap his arms around her torso to stop her. "I'll let you go, but promise me you won't come at me," he said.

The woman didn't agree. They continued to struggle while she continued to hurl abuses at him.

Through her swearing, he heard another woman's voice that sounded familiar. It was the maid named Lakshmi.

"Bhanu," said Lakshmi. "Why did you ask me to come here with your clothes? Where did you—" The other woman's voice broke off in a gasp when she stepped into the room. "Oh my!"

Vishal realized right then that one of his arms was wrapped right around the heaving chest of the struggling half-naked woman and his other arm was wrapped around her bare stomach.

"Get him!" the woman in his arms ordered Lakshmi. "I'm going to kill this worm! Slit his throat and stomp him to death and feed him to our dogs."

Lakshmi appeared calm listening to the younger woman's murderous threats.

"I was told that this is my room," Vishal told Lakshmi while trying to control the struggling woman. "Isn't it?"

"It is," Lakshmi replied. "I have no idea what Bhanu is doing here."

For a moment, the struggles stopped. "You know this worm?" the woman asked Lakshmi.

"He's the new driver."

The woman he held looked shocked. "The driver?"

"Yes."

Taking a deep breath, the woman in his arms hissed out the next words. "Let me go."

Vishal noticed the plump breasts underneath his arm and the softness of the skin on her stomach. Her hair which must have been tied earlier was let loose due to the struggle. Her long hair brushed his hand on her stomach. He wondered how he had ever mistaken her for a boy.

Slowly, he dropped his hands and stepped away from the woman. The woman swung around and glared at him as though she still intended to murder him or at least punch him in his eye. He watched her with an equal amount of wariness and amusement while his eyes couldn't help but wander over her body which was only covered in a bra and jeans.

"Look away, you ass!" she snapped while reaching for the clothes Lakshmi had brought along. "And get out of here and come back much later."

He raised an eyebrow at her rude order but turned to leave the room. Meantime, he heard her frantic voice as she conversed with Lakshmi.

"I went too far this time, Lakshmi. Dinesh and his men are going to come looking for me. If Grandpa asks, tell him I came home on time and was working in the garden with you."

Wondering what the woman had done, Vishal stepped out. He couldn't change out of his travel clothes anywhere, so he headed to Vikram's room to change.

"Didn't like your room?" Vikram asked when he saw Vishal.

"Room is okay. But right now it's occupied by something wild that bites." Vishal grinned, looking down at the back of his hand where there were visible bite marks.

Vikram raised his eyebrow but didn't ask for explanations. "I'm about to step out to grab a meal and meet with Suryaprakash. Want to join?"

"No. I'll skip the meal. I'll just catch some shut-eye in your room." He had barely slept the previous night because of the clubbing.

CHAPTER NINE

Vishal woke up to the sounds of shouting from outside. His watch indicated it was five in the evening. Frowning, he got up from the bed and went out.

There was quite a racket outside the house. Men were shouting, and in between the shouts, Vishal heard the calm and collected voice of Suryaprakash Gulati.

Frowning further, Vishal went to the front of the house. Several people were gathered. Most of them stood outside the gate watching and listening to the spectacle.

In the front yard, there were at least six furious men who were shouting, and one of them was the loudest. "I know she's involved in some way or the other. And she needs to pay for what she did!" The man who said that had a half-shaven head and mustache.

"My hair and my mustache were my pride!" the enraged man continued. "She made me a laughing stock!"

Suryaprakash looked at Lakshmi who was standing at a distance and watching quietly. "Go get Bhanu," he said before turning back to the group of men. "Let's resolve this calmly."

"How can we remain calm?" another man who was standing next to the half-shaven man demanded. "This isn't the first time you and your granddaughters have made a spectacle of us and dragged us to the streets." He turned to look at Sangeeta who had joined her grandfather. "She was supposed to be *my* wife. But you thought I wasn't educated enough for your precious doctor granddaughter and got her married to a nobody from your village." The man had an ugly glint in his eye as he gave her a smug look. "That fool didn't even have enough sense to remain alive to give her a child. Marry me and I'll give you a child within nine months."

Suryaprakash's hands clenched on his walking stick. Vishal was about to intervene, but his brother beat him to it.

"That's enough," Vikram said in a commanding tone. He was standing next to Suryaprakash.

The group of men fell silent all of a sudden and looked at Vikram. Vishal knew even in the garb of modest clothes, Vikram still held an aura of command.

"Who are you?" the man who had been trash talking asked.

"That's none of your business. But if you want to remain here in Mr. Suryaprakash's house, you will keep a civil tongue and show respect to his family."

The men looked like they wanted to argue. But when they saw the glares from the people standing outside, they grudgingly stepped away.

"You called for me, Grandpa?" A sweet voice of a woman interrupted the tension-filled silence.

Vishal turned towards the soft voice and almost choked on his tongue. It was the woman whom he had a confrontation with in the barn room. With most of her clothes on, she looked very different. Especially because she was wearing traditional clothes.

And more than the clothes, the meek attitude was miles away from the aggressive woman who was ready to scratch his eyes out a few hours ago. He somehow knew she was putting on an act, and it amused him. An involuntary laugh escaped him, but he somehow turned it into a cough.

The woman's eyes fell on him, and for a brief moment, he saw a flash in them which promised murder and mayhem before she turned her eyes away from him and looked at her grandfather.

"Bhanu, where were you this afternoon?"

The woman had a confused and puzzled look on her face. "Where I usually am during the weekends, Grandpa. At home. I was in the garden, helping Lakshmi, and later, I was in the barn room, helping clean it." Bhanu's eyes fell on Vishal. "Ask our new driver. He saw me cleaning and even lent me a hand at the end."

Everyone's eyes were on Vishal, and his were on the brazen woman who was watching him with seemingly wide and innocent eyes.

"Yes," he replied in a casual tone. "She was already there almost done cleaning the room."

"I don't believe her!" shouted the half-shaven man. "I know she's lying. She's involved somehow. I just know it. And everyone knows how she is, always butting into others' business!"

The man was about to go to Bhanu threateningly when Vikram stopped him midway. "You have your answer. She said she's not responsible. Now leave."

The man's eyes flared, and he held Vikram's shirt collar. But Vikram didn't budge. He had a cool yet firm look on his face.

Vishal was pissed that someone dared to touch his brother with a violent intention. He marched to the man and dragged him away from Vikram and held the man's shirt. The rest of the men who came with the man surrounded him, but Vishal didn't care. His focus was entirely on the man. He made a fist and pulled his arm back, about to punch the man in the face when Vikram stopped him by putting a hand on his shoulder. "Let him go, Vishal," he said softly.

Glaring at the man, Vishal slowly let go of the man's shirt.

The man huffed and puffed, but seeing the people around him, he again stepped away. "This isn't over," he warned. "I know that it's her."

"You are mistaken that it is Bhanu," said Suryaprakash. "There are so many other people who want to get back at you. It must be one of them."

The man stood silently seething with fury. And the men who had come with him had no choice but to accept things at face value. So with grudging looks, they led the man away.

As soon as the SUV disappeared from sight, Suryaprakash sighed. "Those two men are always out to make trouble for us." He looked at his younger granddaughter. "Dinesh can be dangerous, Bhanu," he said. "I want you to be very careful."

"He's just a hot-headed fool, Grandpa."

"Maybe so. But he and his brother are the types to hold grudges if they think someone did them wrong. I don't feel it's safe for you to be alone when he's around."

Bhanu frowned. "I'm never alone with him. I always have my friends at college."

"No. I meant even when you are driving alone to your college. Or maybe even on the campus." Suryaprakash looked at Vishal. "I want you to drive Bhanu to college for the next few weeks. Stay there with her however late it gets and then return with her."

Vishal nodded. However, Bhanu frowned. "But how will you get around, Grandpa? If the driver is always with me?"

"I know how to drive, too," Vikram replied. "I can drive Mr. Gulati wherever he wants to go."

"Thank you, Vikram. Most of the time, I just walk to the places."

Bhanu wasn't too happy with the idea. "There's no need, Grandpa. I can handle Dinesh—"

"My decision is final." With that, the older man walked away. Using his walking stick, he pushed the gate in front of the house and went outside.

Vishal looked at the Gulati sisters who were still waiting quietly outside.

"Well?" Bhanu Gulati asked, looking at him. "Don't you have somewhere to go, too?"

Vikram had already gone inside the house, probably to the room assigned to him. With a sigh, Vishal followed his brother. Even as he went into Vikram's room, both he and Vikram could still hear the conversation between the Gulati sisters.

"I can't believe this," Bhanu Gulati fumed. "I don't need a damn bodyguard because of such a small incident."

"It's not small, Bhanu," her sister, Sangeeta, said in a serious tone. "You know Dinesh wants to marry you—"

"*Wanted* to marry me," Bhanu corrected. "Not anymore after I set him straight many times."

"Exactly why he's going to want to strike back. I told you many times not to get into trouble with such people."

"Such people should not be ignored. They need to be taught a lesson!"

"And you think the lesson is to steal chloroform from my clinic and shave his hair off while he's unconscious?" Sangeeta asked her younger sister.

"How did you—" Bhanu broke off and cleared her throat. "I have no idea what you're talking about."

Sangeeta sighed. "Just be careful, Bhanu. Make sure you always have Vishal next to you for a few days."

"I can take care of myself. I don't need a caretaker." Bhanu's tone was annoyed. "Least of all him!"

They heard Bhanu storming into the house and going past Vikram's room with her sister, Sangeeta, following behind her with a determined look.

Vishal sighed. "Fucking great!" he said in a tone that only Vikram could hear. "Instead of being Suryaprakash's driver, now I have to waste my time babysitting that bratty woman."

"It'll probably only be for a few days."

"I highly doubt it. That woman is way too aggressive and violent. God knows how many other pissed-off men would be out to get her."

Vikram laughed softly. "Well, best of luck then."

Vishal sighed once again. He really might need the luck.

***

35

Sangeeta followed her younger sister into her room. "Bhanu. You've gone too far this time."

Bhanu sighed. "I know. But it had to be done. I already told you what Dinesh did. He—"

"That doesn't matter. I told you many times that you can't be the avenging angel for everyone and be the one to punish the perpetrators. It's you those guys will be after to take revenge."

Bhanu shook her head tiredly. She had a long day. "Leave it, Geeta. You know I won't change." She smiled at her sister. "Just like you enjoy helping sick people, I enjoy helping people in need."

"Then maybe you should become a lawyer instead of studying to be an engineer. At least then you would be in trouble legitimately."

Bhanu grinned. "Naah. I find lawyers to be too boring."

Sangeeta smiled. "You're right. You are too good of a computer whiz to want to be anything else. Did you open the latest acceptance?"

Bhanu raised her eyebrow. "How are you so sure it's an acceptance?"

"Because, my dear sister, those universities are not stupid. With the website you created for our village and your other successful projects, they have no choice but to jump in excitement to have you study at their universities."

"You're my sister. You're biased."

Sangeeta smiled. "That maybe I am," she said. "But I'm also aware of your ability and true potential. That's why I forced you to apply even though you said you didn't want to pursue higher studies."

"I still don't," Bhanu said softly.

"Not that again!" Sangeeta said with exasperation. "Grandpa and I will be fine here. You need to pursue your dreams."

When Bhanu remained quiet, Sangeeta sighed. "Okay. Let's not argue about that again," she said before giving her younger sister a stern look. "But from tomorrow onwards, I want you to take Vishal with you."

Bhanu frowned. "Ugh! I forgot about them for a moment. Who are those two men, anyway?"

"They came in this morning. They are from the city and want to settle in our village."

"Huh. I don't know about the other guy, but this Vishal guy seems suspicious as hell. Are you sure I would be safer with him than on my own?"

"Bhanu! You better obey Grandpa's orders!"

Bhanu raised her hands in surrender. "Fine. Fine. I will."

Sangeeta got up from the chair. "All right, I'll need to get back to the clinic. See you later."

As soon as Sangeeta left, Bhanu went out of her room to search for her grandfather. She knew he would be worried and had to appease him that she would be fine.

CHAPTER TEN

The next morning, Vishal woke up early. It must be the time lag. Or maybe it was the damn rooster that wouldn't shut up.

Getting out of the bed, he strode outside his room. It was slightly misty outside, but the weather was perfect. Taking a deep breath of fresh air, he got started on the morning routine.

He checked his emails and then exercised for a while before taking a shower. The shower was quick because there was no warm water facility in the bathroom. Something he'd have to get used to for the next few weeks.

Drying himself vigorously, he went to the kitchen for breakfast. Vikram was already in there, checking his emails with a frown.

"Bro, seriously," Vishal said with a grin. He sat on the stool next to Vikram. "You need to stop worrying so much about work. Dad's doing a great job. You need to relax."

"We are not here to relax."

"I know. But constantly worrying about work would just make it all that much harder to think and achieve what we came here for. And it might even prolong our stay here. I don't know about you, but I can't wait to get back to our world where there's damn hot water or at least a proper shower."

Vikram laughed softly. "There's hot water and a shower in the bathroom I'm using."

"Dammit! I should've picked the accountant job."

Before Vikram could reply, a cheerful heavy-set woman who worked as the cook for the Gulatis came in with the breakfast dishes.

Later, after breakfast, Lakshmi gave Vishal the car keys and asked him to wait near the car while Bhanu got ready for college.

Annoyed that he had to wait until her highness got ready, Vishal cooled his heels in the car.

He was checking his emails when there was loud tapping on the window of the car. Raising an eyebrow, he lowered the window to a scowling woman. A scowling beautiful woman.

Bhanu Gulati wore another ethnic dress like the previous day, and the simple red dress hugged her curves in all the right spots. How the hell had he, even for a brief moment, think that she was a boy?

His brain not only threw the visuals of the previous day with her in the state of undress, but it also made him recall how her almost-bare curves felt against his arms.

"Get down," Bhanu said irritably.

His thoughts of the previous day vanished at her tone. "Why?" he asked.

"I want to drive."

He slowly smiled at her. "No."

She appeared stunned. "Did you just say no to me?"

"Your hearing is excellent, Princess," he drawled.

"How dare you say no to me!"

"Quite easily. If you don't want your grandfather to know that you were the one shaving that man's mustache and beard off, you better listen to me and behave."

She went silent for a few seconds. "My grandfather won't believe you," she said finally.

"Want to bet?"

She narrowed her eyes and then a couple of seconds later, throwing him a furious look, she huffed towards the door of the back seat.

"In the front. Come sit next to me," he ordered.

He knew he was pushing it, but he had to set a precedent on how their dynamics would be while he worked as her driver/bodyguard. He loved his grandfather and was willing to do anything for him, but he didn't have to bow down or be deferential to anyone unnecessarily.

He could almost see the fumes coming from her ears and feel the daggers shooting out of her narrowed eyes. But she did as she was told. She sat next to him and closed the door with a loud bang.

Starting the car, he drove out of the gates.

Meantime, Bhanu leaned towards the front and was about to turn on the music on the car stereo when she paused. Vishal could feel her eyes on his hand.

Damn. He knew she was looking at his Rolex watch that his mother had gifted to him on his eighteenth birthday. He wore it always and had felt reluctant to take it off even for the charade.

"That's a Rolex." Her tone was accusatory.

He threw her an amused look. "And?"

"You said you worked as a driver before. I don't believe you."

"Huh. So what's your theory, Princess? That I'm actually a billionaire who chose to come to your village just so I could somehow work for you as your driver and personal bodyguard?"

She scoffed. "No. You hardly look like a billionaire. More like a thief or a conman. I think you stole this watch from someone. And I'm determined to get you caught by—"

"Relax," he cut her off before she got worked up even more. "It's just a cheap knockoff of a Rolex. You can get them at many places in the city. I can get you one, too, if you want."

She seemed slightly appeased. "No thanks," she said in a snooty tone.

Then ignoring him completely, she turned on the music on the car stereo. Surprisingly her highness liked Indian classical music.

An hour later, after several curt instructions of the directions, her highness finally asked him to stop outside the gates of the university campus.

"Wait for me here. I don't want to come out and keep looking or waiting for you." She fished out something from her purse. It was money. "For your lunch. There are many food options that are close by." She didn't even bother handing the money over. She kept it on the dashboard and stepped out.

Vishal stared at the woman with narrowed eyes as she walked away with her long hair swinging against her backside and disappeared inside the gates. His fingers itched to spank that perky butt.

***

Bhanu was annoyed.

She couldn't believe that her new driver had the gall to blackmail her. And it was a damn big blackmail because she loved her grandfather a lot, and she hated being the cause of his disappointment.

She had to get rid of the current driver somehow.

The damn man not only knew her secret, but he even got an eyeful when she was changing her clothes. It was beyond embarrassing, even though at that time, she was too furious at him to bother about her undressed state.

Maybe it was her imagination, but when his eyes fell on her this morning, she felt as though he was recalling how she looked half-naked.

She really had to get rid of him!

"Bhanu!" one of her friends, Kavita, shouted from a distance.

Bhanu's eyes fell on the group of giggling girls who were waiting for her in their usual meeting spot under a large tree.

"Hey, girls," she greeted.

"Did you see Dinesh today?" Kavita asked.

"Not yet. Why?" Bhanu asked.

"He came in with a fake mustache and wig. He looks ridiculous!" There was loud laughter.

Bhanu grinned. "I don't think any girl will fall for his trap anytime soon."

Her friends laughed once again.

And then, someone gasped.

"Oh my God!" said Kavita. "Who's that! I would fall for his trap anytime!" Kavita's voice held a note of awe.

Frowning, Bhanu turned to see whom her friends were gawking at.

It was Vishal, and he was walking towards her group or rather swaggering her way.

"Who are you girls talking about?" Bhanu asked. "I just see an ass." She was deliberately loud enough for him to hear. But the bastard just smiled and then grinned when he noticed the group of girls watching him with wide eyes.

There were more gasps. "Sweet God! He has dimples!" Kavita exclaimed.

Bhanu was quite sure he let his dimples out deliberately. *Not that I had noticed them or care about them*, she hurriedly thought.

"Bahh. They are just indentations on a face. Get over it." Bhanu turned to the still grinning man. "What?" she snapped. "Didn't I ask you to not step out of the car unless it's absolutely needed?"

"You forgot your lunch, Princess." He handed her the bag that Lakshmi packed for her.

She pulled the bag from his hands. "Stop calling me that name!"

"Then stop behaving like an entitled princess," he rejoined. "And you forgot to thank me. For driving you here and also for getting you the lunch bag."

The rest of the girls were watching the exchange with shock-filled widened eyes. Bhanu took a deep breath and controlled herself.

"Well? I'm waiting," he said, testing her control and patience further.

Taking another deep breath, "Thank you," she gritted out. "Now go! Wait near the car!"

Giving her another amused raised eyebrow, he strode away.

"Who is he!" Kavita demanded to know as soon as he left.

"My new driver."

Everyone looked even more shocked.

"Are you sure he's a driver?" Kavita asked. "And had it been any other man speaking to you like that, you would've bitten off his head."

"Yes, he's a driver. He's new and needs to work on his attitude. But don't worry, he'll be fired or he'll pack up and leave on his own before the week is gone." Bhanu intended to fulfill that vow sooner than later.

CHAPTER ELEVEN

Vikram had a relatively uneventful morning. He was used to waking up and jumping right into his phone calls, so it felt odd with all the free time on his hands.

He had woken up to the sounds of a classical musical instrument. He thought it was a music recording played by someone inside the house, but he was pleasantly surprised that Sangeeta was the one playing the instrument. She was playing it for her grandfather.

Vikram watched her play while he waited to speak with the older man. When Sangeeta was done playing, Vikram went to Suryaprakash. "Sir, do you have some time to show me the accounts?"

Suryaprakash smiled. "I'm in a hurry today because of the cutting season. But I've asked our bank accountant to come by and help you." He looked at the large Grandfather clock on the wall. "All right, I'll see you later. I should be back in the afternoon."

With that, the older man left the house.

It was still only eight o'clock and Vikram didn't know what to do. Vishal had left and would most likely return in the evening.

Sighing, he went out of the house to explore the place. Immediately, his eyes fell on the long line of people who were waiting outside the small clinic.

"Why are there so many people?" Vikram asked Kailash who had just come out of the clinic. Vikram had met Kailash earlier and knew that he was Sangeeta's assistant.

"Monday morning," Kailash replied. "Doctor Madam holds a free clinic."

"I see."

"Can you wait inside the clinic, just in case Doctor Madam calls for me?" Kailash requested. "I'll need to grab some supplies from the house."

"Sure." Vikram went inside the clinic and waited.

He could see Sangeeta with her patients. She was looking at a middle-aged man in a stern manner. "The next time I hear that you operated the grass-cutting machine while you were drunk, I'll personally come and chop your leg off. Understood?" she said.

The man looked shamefaced and nodded.

"Now go. Take rest and spend time with your wife and son. Your wife was complaining to me the other day that you barely go home and just hang around the centre to get drunk."

"I won't do it again," the man replied in a small voice.

Sangeeta smiled and waved at him. As soon as that man left, another patient went in without even a minute's pause. Sangeeta greeted the woman with a smile before beginning to question her about her ailment. And while she checked the patient's heartbeat, she began to converse about the patient's family.

Vikram found her intriguing.

Suryaprakash's last accountant whose job Vikram was currently filling in for, had informed that Suryaprakash would soon be on the verge of filing bankruptcy. Suryaprakash had apparently donated most of his lands and lent money to people without even asking for interest. The old man and his granddaughters only lived from a modest income that came from the rice mills and agriculture.

But still, the woman in front of him had a ready natural smile on her face as she treated the patients for free.

He didn't know much about her because he was only interested to know everything about the man he had come to impress. But now, he wanted to know a little about Sangeeta.

As though the object of his thoughts could sense his gaze, she looked in his direction. Her smile widened, transforming her pretty face to appear breathtakingly beautiful. Before he could react or respond, Kailash returned to the clinic. "Thanks, Vikram. The accountant is here looking for you. He said he came in early as he has to leave soon."

Pushing away the strange thoughts of wanting to know more about Sangeeta, Vikram decided to focus on the task at hand and the ultimate goal. He had no time or couldn't afford to be distracted by a bright-eyed, beautiful woman.

Six hours later, after Vikram finally could get hold of the account books and the bank statements, he was going through Suryaprakash's finances item by item. The bank manager had spent only a few minutes with Vikram walking through everything before leaving for his job.

The background check report on Suryaprakash was right. Suryaprakash was way too generous, more than he could afford. And not only was the generosity working against the older man, the previous accountant who had recently left was also taking advantage by stealing from him.

Vikram was determined to send a message to Pooja to get hold of the accountant and make him return the money he stole from the older man. The amount the man was given to quit his job more than compensated for it.

"Vikram?" a soft feminine voice called.

Vikram looked up from the accounting books to the smiling face of Sangeeta.

"Have you had your lunch?" she asked.

"Not yet."

"Then come. Join me. Kamala is going to complain about me having lunch this late. I might as well have you with me as company to share the grumbling."

The clock on the wall indicated that it was close to two thirty in the afternoon. "Let's go," he said with a small smile.

They sat outside on a cemented structure in the middle of the courtyard under a large tree.

"Is Mr. Suryaprakash back?"

"No. Grandpa mostly takes a packed lunch to the mill."

"I see." He looked at the woman who was serving food onto his plate from a packed lunch carrier. "What about you? It's quite late for lunch."

She finished serving and sat back with a smile. "Yes, Mondays are usually like this because of the free clinic. I only take a quick thirty-minute break and see patients until six in the evening. The rest of the days are not this crazy."

She began to serve food onto her plate. "What about you?" she asked with a laugh. "Did our accounts spin your head yet? Bhanu and I used to help Grandpa with the accounts until a few years ago before we got too busy with studies and practice."

"I'm not used to seeing accounts on actual paper books. Usually, most companies and even private parties use computers."

"I know! But Grandpa insists on having accounts written in books, even though he doesn't have enough time to check them himself. Hopefully, you can convince him to have the accounts entered on a computer."

"I will."

Barely fifteen minutes had passed since she took the break, but she was eating hurriedly.

"The population of this village isn't that big. Do people from the neighboring villages also avail the services of the free clinic?"

She laughed. "No. It's just people from my village. Most of them are fine. But they feel the need to get themselves checked often to make use of the free clinic. I don't mind because I have Kailash helping me prioritize the seriousness of the ailments."

She finished the rest of her food hurriedly before getting up. "Sorry to leave while you're still eating. I need to go before my patients begin to fight outside the clinic." She smiled and waved him goodbye before hurrying away.

Vikram watched until Sangeeta disappeared around the corner where her clinic was situated.

It felt odd. Usually, Vikram was the one hurrying through lunch or always on the run because of his lifestyle. And now he was rusticating in a village, and the woman who was beginning to intrigue him zipped around hardly having time to even sit for a leisurely meal.

He went back to the accounts after lunch.

Suryaprakash returned home at four. Unlike the previous accountant, Vikram made it a point to set the precedent of spending as much time as possible with him. He began speaking to the older man about the accounts and used that as the pretext to be with him more often.

"I would like to join you so I can see everything and get an idea of the revenue the mills and your crops are making."

Suryaprakash nodded. "I'll take you with me starting next week. I don't usually go often. But since this is the crop-cutting time, I like to oversee things." The older man sipped on the tea that was served to him by Lakshmi. "How did you like your first day so far?" he asked.

Vikram took a sip from his cup before answering. "It's going to take a few days to get the accounts in order and understand them. I would recommend putting them on a computer while I go through them thoroughly."

Suryaprakash frowned. "I like going through the accounts myself sometimes. But I'm too old to learn computers at my age."

"There's no need to learn the computers. I can just print it and present the accounts to you whenever you want. It's just easy to maintain them there."

The older man hesitated a little before he nodded. "Okay. Buy something that isn't too expensive."

Vikram had already sent instructions to Pooja earlier that morning. A top of the line laptop which looked unassuming was going to be shipped along with a printer and delivered the next morning.

"I wasn't talking about just work," said Suryaprakash. "Do you need anything to settle in?"

"No. My brother and I are comfortable."

"Good. Sundays are your free days. We have the Banni festival coming up. I'm too old for joining the festivities, but you and your brother should go. You can explore the village and also see how we village people enjoy ourselves."

"We definitely will," said Vikram.

Vikram chatted with the older man for more time until the older man retired into his room to rest.

Later in the evening, when it was almost eight, Vishal came by to his room.

"Had dinner?" Vishal asked.

"Not yet. I was waiting for you."

"I'm famished. Let's go."

As soon as they went into the kitchen, the cook readied two plates filled with food. They carried their plates outside and sat in the backyard that offered them enough privacy.

"Is the University far from here?" Vikram asked.

"No. It's just an hour's ride away. But that damn woman made me stop at four other places and disappeared for hours together. Anyway, were you able to speak with Suryaprakash?"

"A little. He's apparently busy this week."

While they had their meal, they strategized ways to be able to spend a decent enough time with Suryaprakash.

Much later, when they went back to their assigned rooms, Vikram recalled his conversation with Suryaprakash. The older man seemed to be quite reasonable and understanding.

Vikram wondered what had happened to make such a man dig in his feet and hold on to a grudge towards his childhood friend.

CHAPTER TWELVE

The next few days followed the similar pattern. Each day, Vishal left in the morning with Bhanu while Vikram worked on the accounts and spent some time with Suryaprakash in the evenings.

They weren't spending much time with the older man, but they made use of the time trying to impress the older man with their work.

Vishal was currently outside the university campus. He was firing off yet another email while talking on the headset to one of the VPs when there was a knock on the car window.

Bhanu had returned, and she had the annoyed frown on her face that she had whenever she saw him. Ending his call, Vishal unlocked the door.

Bhanu hurriedly got in and threw a glance outside.

Vishal saw a guy running towards the car. Frowning and thinking that the man was out to harm her, Vishal got out of the car.

"Where are you going?" Bhanu asked. "Come back here and let's go!" she ordered.

Vishal ignored her. He braced himself for an attack and a fight. But upon closer look, the man running towards the car didn't seem menacing. In fact, he appeared frantic and desperate.

"Bhanu!" the man shouted. "Please. I love you! Tell me you'll marry me! Otherwise, I'm going to kill myself!"

Vishal frowned. Meantime, instead of looking worried or nervous, Bhanu seemed exasperated and annoyed. *Did all men exasperate and annoy her?*

"How can you not accept my proposal, Bhanu?" the man asked in an anguished tone. "I wrote all of my feelings in blood for you!"

Bhanu rolled her eyes. "If I accepted the proposal of every guy who wrote me letters with their blood, I'd probably be married well over a dozen times. And stop writing with blood. It's unhygienic and disgusting."

Vishal raised an amused eyebrow at the exchange. Bhanu turned towards him. "What are you waiting for?" she snapped. "Get inside the car and let's go!"

Shaking his head, Vishal went back towards the driver's seat and slid in. As he started the car, the man's loud shouts could be heard.

"I'm not giving up on my love, Bhanu! I'll keep on trying until my dying day!"

"Great," she muttered. "Another idiot following me everywhere I go."

"Too many love-sick puppies trailing behind you, Princess?" Vishal asked while he reversed the car to drive out of the campus parking lot.

Bhanu threw him an annoyed look. "Mind your business. And next time I ask you to start the car, you start the car. Understand?"

"Sure, Princess."

"I told you to stop calling me that!"

"Okay... Princess."

Vishal grinned hearing the woman next to him huff out in annoyance.

He realized that he liked getting a rise out of her. And it was way too easy with her fiery nature. He knew he should tone it down, but he didn't want to. One of the main reasons was because he was onto her. He knew she desperately wanted to get rid of him or make him quit the driver's job on his own.

And the way she went about to achieve her goal was amusing. Over the past few days, whenever she returned from her classes, they never went straight home. She made him stop at every possible place. And each time, she didn't bother telling him where she was going or how long she would be gone. She simply disappeared into people's houses and came back again to give him more instructions on where they would be going next. Sometimes, her university friends joined her. He was made to drive around her friends to do some of their chores. It was only mildly annoying but immensely amusing because he knew it was her juvenile attempt to make him quit.

That evening Bhanu made him stop at a hospital first. And by the time she came out, it was almost dark, and they finally headed back.

"Wait. Stop the car!" she ordered.

They were in the middle of nowhere with just large trees and farmlands around them. "Now what? There's no one here to meet," he said.

"Just stop!" she snapped.

He stepped on the brake pedal until she jerked forward. Throwing him a dirty look, she stepped out. And then, she began searching the ground. A few moments later, she picked up a medium-sized stick and marched determinedly towards a large tree.

He stepped out of the car and followed her with a frown. *Now what is she up to?*

Behind the large tree there was a faint glow of fire. When he took a few more steps behind her, he saw that surrounding the fire were half-a-dozen men sitting and drinking.

As soon as one of them saw Bhanu, they alerted each other. "Bhanu! Oh my God, it's Bhanu! Run!"

They all scrambled up and swayed in a drunken stupor.

Bhanu raised the stick. "It's the cutting season, and you men are getting drunk? How many times should I warn you?" she shouted.

"Banni festival is coming up..." a man began to reason.

"So? That doesn't give you an excuse to drink and endanger your lives and make your families suffer!" She went at them with the stick.

The men, although drunk, were quick on their legs. They began running away not bothering to pick the belongings they left under the tree.

"Drunken idiots," she muttered.

When she turned back and saw him, her frown grew. "Who asked you to follow behind me?" she demanded.

Vishal shook his head with a slow grin. "I'm supposed to be protecting you," he said. "But I can see that the men from your village need more protection from *you*."

She responded by tossing her long hair back and walking towards the car. And then, she ignored him completely while they drove back home.

***

As soon as Bhanu entered the house, she saw that her grandfather and sister were already waiting for her at the dinner table.

"Grandpa! I've told you many times not to wait for me," she scolded.

Suryaprakash smiled. "And I told you that this is the only time we get to spend with each other as a family."

Sangeeta greeted Bhanu before serving food for the three of them. Bhanu jumped right into her meal as she felt famished after a long day.

"How was your day?" Sangeeta asked reading her mind.

"Long." And made even longer because of an annoying man whose presence in the last few days rubbed her the wrong way. The guy was way too arrogant and cocky while constantly passing smartass remarks.

"Grandpa, I think we should look for an alternative driver. The man you hired recently isn't good."

Suryaprakash Gulati seemed surprised. "Why? Vikram and Vishal both seem decent and hardworking."

"We shouldn't simply trust them at their face value, Grandpa."

"It isn't just their face value. Vikram is quite good at what he does. He was able to put all of our finances together in a matter of days."

Sangeeta remained quiet through the exchange.

Bhanu pushed a little harder. "But his younger brother isn't good at his job. He drives way too fast and—"

Sangeeta laughed. "Faster than you?"

Her sister had a point. "Yes. And he's too meddlesome—"

"He's supposed to be meddlesome, Bhanu," Sangeeta stated. "Especially if Dinesh or his men try to bother you."

"Geeta is right, Bhanu. And besides, even though I didn't get a chance to speak much to that boy, what I have seen of him so far, he seems respectable enough and even helps out without being asked. It's not part of his duties, but the other day, he helped our people unload the heavy grain bags and carried them inside the barn."

Bhanu was frustrated. Why was everyone so taken in by him? Even her friends who were supposed to help her get rid of him, ended up chatting and laughing with him when he drove them around.

It was intolerable that he was getting away with so much because of his blackmail. No more. She was determined to get rid of him once and for all. Hopefully, the Banni festival that was coming up would offer her a better chance.

CHAPTER THIRTEEN

Vikram and Vishal were inside the barn, talking to their father on the speaker phone. The rest of the household was busy with the preparations of the Banni festival which was supposed to begin early next morning.

"How's everything, Dad?" Vikram asked over the phone.

"Everything is fine here," Rajesh Saaho replied. "Just take care of yourselves."

"When did the doctors say Grandfather will be able to talk?" Vishal asked.

"So far they want him to rest. And your mom does, too. She thinks he's made to rest for all the years of restless work he's done."

Vishal smiled. "Trust Mum to put a positive spin on everything."

Rajesh Saaho agreed. "So any luck yet with having personal talks with Suryaprakash?"

"No. Not yet," said Vikram. "But we will soon. I'm spending some time each day with him, but not enough. After this week, I'll be able to be with him more."

"Good."

They spoke for a few more minutes before Vikram ended the call. He sighed. "It's already been a week. We really need to figure out a way to impress Suryaprakash."

"I know," Vishal said in frustration. "So far I haven't much inkling or direct contact with Suryaprakash. All because of that bratty woman who by the way is busier than any damn prime minister of a country. You have no idea how many damn people she knows in this tiny freaking place. And I'm running her errands and babysitting her rather than charming the old man."

Vikram raised an eyebrow. "I'm spending enough time with Mr. Suryaprakash." He had a small amused smile. "Maybe you should charm the younger granddaughter, so she can help us convince her grandfather in the future."

Vishal had a horrified look. "Charm that she-devil? I doubt anyone can ever charm her. I think she hates all men under sixty."

Vikram smiled with amusement. "Can't believe that Vishal Saaho, the well-known charmer is saying that."

"Laugh it away, big brother," said Vishal with a mock grudging look. "I can finally rest a bit. I don't have to drive her highness around for a few days."

Vikram smiled. Currently, Srirampur and the surrounding villages were geared up to participate in the Banni festival. It was supposedly one of the biggest celebrated festivals around the area. Not only Suryaprakash, but also other people were telling Vikram about the event. Including Sangeeta.

Vikram's thoughts were filled by the older granddaughter of the man he had come to impress. Just like they had been the entire week.

Each day, after spending a few hours going through the accounts and sending the pictures of the transactions so that Pooja could get someone to enter them into the system, Vikram and Sangeeta had lunch together. They had casual conversations where mostly Sangeeta was the one chatting.

Sangeeta told him about the village and its people in general. It wasn't anything groundbreaking, but he liked listening to her speak animatedly with so much interest and zeal towards her people and village. Sometimes, she invited Kailash or some other help to join them for lunch. But those men were reluctant.

Vikram knew the class system was ingrained into many people in not only the rural area but also the urban cities of India. It wasn't the norm that Sangeeta had no qualms of having lunch with her accountant. He liked that about her. She was friendly and treated everyone as an equal.

Vikram also found Sangeeta's coping to her tragic past quite intriguing. According to the investigative reports that Pooja had briefed him the previous night, Sangeeta Gulati was married nearly a year ago. And her husband of two days had died in a car accident. At that time, he had been heading to a hospital in the city for a conference. But since Sangeeta had a last-minute emergency call with a patient, she had gone in another car with her younger sister and grandfather.

It was indeed quite tragic.

Over the last few days, Vikram had spent nearly an hour listening to everything that was gathered about Sangeeta in the investigative reports. And when Pooja offered to brief him with information on Sangeeta's younger sister, he told her it wasn't needed.

A long silence had followed on the line. Vikram didn't care and neither did he feel the need to explain to Pooja why he was interested to know everything about just Sangeeta in particular.

He didn't know the reason either. He just knew he did.

Vikram's thoughts were interrupted by the loud sounds of conch shells. It was followed by the rhythmic beat of drums.

"I think the festivities are starting," said Vishal.

Sangeeta had mentioned to Vikram that the beginning of the festival was kicked off from the Gulati house according to tradition.

"Let's go join them," he said. "If we are to convince that we're interested to settle down in this village, we should look and act interested."

Vishal and he went to the front of the house where the rest of the household along with at least a hundred people were gathered. Most of them had fire-lit torches and were holding long bamboo sticks with colored cloths tied to the ends.

As the rousing drumbeats continued, Suryaprakash was making several offerings to the goddess statue in the form of flowers, food and also the harvested grains. Meantime, his younger granddaughter lit more lamps and placed them near the god.

Vikram's eyes automatically sought out Sangeeta. He found her standing back along with the rest of the household. She had a demure look as she watched the procession.

As though she felt his eyes on her, she looked towards him. And as their eyes met, she smiled. As usual, her smile brightened her face and everything around her.

Vikram didn't smile back and continued to watch her even as the procession began to move.

"Coming?" Vishal asked.

"No. You go ahead. I'll join tomorrow. I'll stay here with Suryaprakash."

Vikram continued to watch Sangeeta as she and Suryaprakash went back into the house while the rest of the household joined the procession. He knew that the people would all leave to go to the temple grounds where events would be held over the next two days.

Vikram went inside the house to speak with Suryaprakash, and found the older man arguing with his granddaughter.

"You're not old like me, Geeta. You should go and join the festivities along with the rest of the young people."

"I'm not leaving you alone at home, Grandpa. And besides, I'll go later when the stick fights begin."

"I'm not going to be alone. Lakshmi and the rest of the household are going to be here with me. They'll join you to watch the stick fights while I'm resting."

Sangeeta looked uncertain. The older man looked exasperated. When he noticed Vikram's presence, his eyes brightened. "Vikram, you're right on time, my boy," he said. "Geeta will show you how we celebrate and have fun in our village."

"I'm—" Before Sangeeta could argue further, her grandfather cut her off.

"Geeta. Vikram won't be able to go on his own. Who better an ambassador for our village than you?"

"Grandpa!" Geeta said with a laugh. "You're impossible." She turned to Vikram who was standing silently. "I'll grab my purse and be right back," she said with a smile.

Even though the plan of staying back to use the opportunity to get closer to Suryaprakash was derailed, Vikram didn't mind. In fact, strangely enough, he was looking forward to spending the day in Sangeeta's company.

***

The celebration for the Banni festival continued. The entire village was decorated using long sticks with pieces of various colored cloths tied to them. People from the surrounding villages were also attending the festivities.

Sangeeta took Vikram around the temple fairgrounds. Devotional music floated through the air while folk-dancing and singing continued on the side. The entire place was crowded and buzzing with activity.

Several stalls of ethnic crafts, games and food were set up. Most of them were makeshift cloth booths which required the visitors to stand outside and shop. There was boisterous laughter from the games booths and argent haggling in the ones where goods were sold.

Sangeeta smiled, loving every second of it. She looked at Vikram who was taking in everything very quietly. "Is this your first time attending a village fair?" she asked.

Vikram looked at her and nodded. "Yes," he said. "I've attended fairs in the various cities with my parents and brother, but even those seem like they were quite a long time ago."

Sangeeta heard and sensed his nostalgia. She was curious to know more about this silent, dignified man. She wanted to ask him about his childhood and his family, but she knew now wasn't the time.

"You and your brother have come to the right place to settle down. We, the people from Srirampur, take our entertainment very seriously. We have village fairs almost once every three months. But this is the biggest of all."

His eyes looked amused. "Looks like you're taking the role of being the ambassador of Srirampur quite seriously, Doctor Sangeeta."

Sangeeta burst out laughing. "Oh, that's another job that I'm passionate about, too." Before she could add more, people continued to pour in. She was about to get jostled, but she felt him put his arm around her waist. He used his broad shoulders to guide her out of the way.

Sangeeta knew that it was a casual gesture on his part to simply protect her from getting pushed around in the heavy crowd. But she felt stunned by how natural and right it seemed to have his arm around her. Luckily, even though the villagers were a conservative lot, in the festive mood no one really seemed to notice or care that he was touching her.

"So, where do you want to go first?" she asked him.

He didn't answer her. He led her towards the stalls that were serving food.

She was surprised. "It's only ten. Are you hungry already?" she asked him.

"Not me. You," he replied. "You skipped your dinner because you had to go for someone's childbirth. And then, when you got back, you were busy helping with the preparations until this morning."

Sangeeta smiled. "Ah. So Grandpa recruited you into his team to complain about my eating habits."

"Yes."

She burst out laughing again. "Fine. I'm hungry, and these wonderful smells are making me feel like I'm starving."

He took her to the place where they were serving huge *dosas*. She was surprised that he noticed and even bothered to remember that it was her favorite food. He paid for and brought a plate with a dosa that was as long as her arm.

She dug in immediately. By the time she looked up, she had devoured three-fourths of it. She saw a small smile play on his lips which made her grin. "You probably must think of me as a glutton."

"No. I think of you as one of those rare lucky people, who despite their busy lives, manage to take the time to enjoy their food. Food for many is just a fuel."

She laughed. "I got it from my grandmother. My grandfather tells me that Bhanumati Gulati took her food and cooking very seriously."

"When did your grandmother pass away?" he asked.

"A few months before Bhanu was born. Bhanu was named after her."

"I see."

The sounds of the conch shell and drums from the morning were heard once again. And the buzz of activity seemingly increased, and most people began to go towards the open area in front of the temple.

Sangeeta quickly wiped her hands on a clean tissue. "The fights are going to start. The stick fights are the highlight of the festival. I don't want you to miss them. Let's go!"

They followed the crowd which began to gather in a circle. But since she was a doctor, she was allowed to stand in the front. She grabbed Vikram's hand and pulled him in the front to stand next to her.

CHAPTER FOURTEEN

Vishal was enjoying himself. Despite being used to the fast life in various cities across the world, he still found the ambiance and festivities of the village sweetly enticing.

Or maybe it was the alcohol in his system that made him feel great.

"You're so lucky, Vishal. You get to spend a lot of time in Bhanu's company. Tell us what Bhanu likes."

He was in the company of half a dozen men who were university students attending the festivities. And all of them belonged to a self-proclaimed club called 'Bhanu's Fanclub.' They had recognized him as most of them saw him waiting outside their university campus.

Soon, they managed to lure him to join their group by tempting him with alcohol. The drinks served currently were definitely not the top quality ones that he was used to. But beggars couldn't be choosers. So he simply joined them.

And the current topic was enough to make him reach out for another drink.

"Bhanu is decidedly the most beautiful woman in the whole world!" one fanboy said in his drunken stupor.

There were loud murmurs of agreement.

The rest of the fanboys didn't want to lag behind and began to wax-poetic about her beautiful eyes, smile and even her damn nose.

Vishal heard enough. "She's not that beautiful," he rejoined.

The fan boys looked scandalized.

"You're joking!" one guy said. "Are you saying you don't find Bhanu beautiful?"

Vishal frowned. He became quite pissed that despite thinking the woman was a brat, he did find her attractive as hell. Not just beauty since he has been used to beautiful women. Hell, he even dated a few Miss Worlds and actresses who were more than stunning. But something about the way Bhanu was always filled with passion whenever she was angry or happy pulled him towards her.

And it hurt his damn ego that the object of his attraction barely acknowledged his presence. To her, he was a lowly employee who only annoyed her at best.

"Eh, Bhanu is just average looking," he said. "Her mouth is too wide, her eyes are way too big and her nose is too small. A shit ton lot of plastic surgery, she might eventually look somewhat beautiful. Even then, with her attitude, no sane man will ever willingly want to fall or associate himself romantically to her."

There were gasps and everyone stood up all of a sudden. Vishal blinked away the pleasant haze to see why they all stood up. He didn't tell something that shocking.

And then, he knew why. Bhanu was standing right there at a distance, looking furious. She was with some of her university girlfriends.

"You guys are drinking," she spat as though drinking was the vilest of all the vices.

"Sorry, B-Bhanu," one of the guys stammered out. "I-I didn't want to drink, these guys forced me. I know you hate drinking."

"Don't lie!" said another guy. "These guys forced me to drink, Bhanu. Even I hate anyone who drinks alcohol."

Vishal shook his head at their pathetic attempts. "Guys, guys," he drawled. "There's no need to lie or give explanations. We have every right to celebrate the way we want to." He threw Bhanu a challenging smile.

"And we want to celebrate by getting piss drunk. Isn't that right, guys?" he continued.

But there were no responses. "Guys?" he asked and turned around. He saw the backs of the men fleeing from the place in staggering movements.

"Cowards," he muttered before turning back to her.

Bhanu continued to glare at him.

"You don't scare me, Princess," he said. Despite his attempt, his voice was slightly slurred. "And you need to stop scaring the poor, hapless men around here. Pretty soon, I'm going to make sure they learn to stand up to your bullying."

She scoffed. "If you remain here for that long," she said with a determined look.

Shaking his head, Vishal picked up a bottle of water and poured it on top of his head. Whatever the hell was in that alcohol, it gave one hell of a kick.

The sound of conch shells along with the rhythmic beats of drums began once again. He saw people at a distance heading somewhere in a hurry.

"Where are they going?" he asked, surprised that she still stood there and didn't storm away as usual.

"The stick fighting event is going to begin." She was watching him speculatively. "It's the main event of the festival. You should join us."

Vishal was surprised once again at her invitation which wasn't made in her usual rude or annoyed tone. Maybe it was because her friends were next to her. "Fine. Lead the way, Princess," he said.

When his legs wavered, and he almost bumped into her from behind, she turned and wrinkled her nose. "You reek of alcohol," she said in disgust.

"That's because I just drank alcohol."

Instead of anger and further disgust, he saw a satisfied smile on her face which was all the more confusing.

Now, what is the brat up to?

CHAPTER FIFTEEN

Large groups of men hit at each other's heads using their long sticks. Some of the groups had two men standing in the centre while deflecting the blows from the group. There were a few casualties. A group of nurses along with a small group of doctors which included Sangeeta were at the sidelines attending to the injured men right away.

Bhanu, along with her friends and also Vishal, joined Sangeeta and Vikram.

When the two men fighting with the group deflected yet another blow, people cheered wildly. But eventually two against ten became too much, and they gave up.

"Next fight is even more exciting. It's one man against six. And the man who offered to fight is a newcomer."

At the announcement, there was palpable excitement among the crowd as they wondered who the newcomer was who was challenging to combat six experienced fighters.

Bhanu turned and let a deliberate smile at Vishal. "That would be you," she said.

Vishal frowned. "What?"

"You will be accepted into Srirampur with open arms if you participate in this fight whether you win or not."

"Bhanu!" Sangeeta interrupted. "What are you doing? He might get seriously hurt. Even the ones who have been practicing over the years end up injured."

"I'm not forcing him, Geeta. I'm just saying that since he came to build a life here in our village, perhaps this will prove to everyone he's serious." She smirked at Vishal who was continuing to watch her with a frown. "You know how to fight, don't you? After all, you're supposed to be protecting me."

Sangeeta pulled at Bhanu's hand. "Bhanu! Stop this childishness right now. Stop goading him."

"I can protect you just fine, Princess," Vishal replied maintaining their eye contact. "And I know how to fight with sticks," he added.

Bhanu's smile grew wider. "See," she told her sister. "He said he can fight." She indicated to Kailash. "Get Vishal a stick made of the finest wood."

A long stick was handed to Vishal. Staring at it and blinking rapidly as though to clear his vision, Vishal took the stick and slowly walked towards the circle of fighters.

Bhanu frowned when she noticed that Vishal held the stick in a surprisingly good position. Maybe he picked it up while watching the previous fights.

"Bhanu, you know this isn't right," Sangeeta said in an urgent tone.

"Relax, Geeta. It's just the men who work in our fields who are sparring right now. You know Grandpa doesn't allow them to use the metal tips. At most, they'll rough him up a little. He's going to be fine."

The fighting began. Bhanu was reluctantly impressed. For a city dweller and a thoroughly drunk one at that, Vishal was doing a good job warding off the blows. Four more men joined the circle and attacked him, but still, he continued to ward off the blows.

A couple of minutes passed until he couldn't ward off a blow. And surprisingly, instead of bruising, he was bleeding due to the wound on his temple.

Bhanu frowned. Instead of taking turns to attack the man at the center, quite a few men were attacking Vishal at the same time.

"Bhanu!" Sangeeta said in an urgent tone. "They are not just our men. I see Dinesh and his men too. And some of them are using metal tips underneath the cloth!"

Bhanu took her eyes off of Vishal and looked at the men attacking him. Sangeeta was right. Dinesh and his men had joined the circle.

"Stop!" Sangeeta shouted at the men.

At Sangeeta's instruction, the men from their village stopped, but Dinesh's men continued to attack Vishal.

"They are not stopping. They might kill him!" Sangeeta said in a panic-laden tone.

Bhanu took the stick lying on the ground and was just about to go into the circle, but Sangeeta stopped her. "Bhanu, these are guys who have a grudge against you. They're not going to listen to you or go easy on you. They'll even attack you along with him."

"There's no other alternative, Geeta. I'll have to try and stop them before they possibly commit a murder."

"You don't have to go," Bhanu heard a voice say. It was Vishal's brother, Vikram.

"Sangeeta is right, it's dangerous for you. I'll go," he said.

"Vikram. It's dangerous for you, too," Sangeeta said in an urgent tone. "I'll go get the police. They're supposed to be where there are ongoing fights. Dinesh must have asked them to leave."

"I'll be fine," he replied quietly.

Sangeeta threw him a worried look before hurrying off to get the police. Bhanu wanted to join her. But she stayed in case she was needed or had to join Vishal's brother to help break up the fight.

***

Vikram went to the place where the spare sticks were kept. Instead of one, he picked up three long sticks. He then went towards the fight where Vishal was barely holding on trying to ward off the blows by aggressive attackers.

The fight slowed briefly and everyone's eyes were on Vikram.

"You know how it's done," Vikram told his brother throwing him another stick.

Vishal took a deep breath and closed his eyes briefly, before opening them again with a determined look. "It's been a while, but damn right I know how it's done," he replied.

And then, both the brothers stood with their backs facing each other with the rapidly twirling sticks. This time, all men surrounding them came at them at the same time. Vikram and Vishal could not easily deflect the blows but also attack them with the sticks.

It took less than fifteen minutes. Soon, Dinesh and his men lay on the ground, no longer able to fight. People from the villages cheered the victory of the newcomers rather than Dinesh and his men.

CHAPTER SIXTEEN

"That dratted woman almost got me killed. Someone should've spanked the hell out of her when she was a child. Maybe then she wouldn't be such a spoiled brat. I'm almost tempted to drag her out of the house and do it myself!"

Vishal and Vikram were inside Vishal's room. After the fight that afternoon, the police finally intervened and gave a strict warning to Dinesh and his people. While the rest of the festivities continued, Vikram and Vishal returned home along with Sangeeta and Bhanu.

Vikram was about to tell Vishal not to do anything rash when he felt a presence.

It was the maid, Lakshmi. She had come with a food carrier and a small bag.

"Medicines and food for you both," she said, placing the things on the small table next to the bed.

Lakshmi looked at Vikram. "Sangeeta asked me to bring even your meal here. She said you might choose to stay by your brother."

"Yes. I'll be here for a while. Thank you and please thank Sangeeta as well."

Vikram waited for Lakshmi to leave, but the woman was watching them closely.

"Is there anything else?" Vikram asked.

She smiled. "Your grandfather taught you both how to fight pretty well. I didn't think his interest would remain even after moving to London."

There was utter silence.

Vishal cleared his throat before replying. "I don't know what you are talking about," he said.

Lakshmi smiled. "Vishwanath Saaho was one of the best fighters this village had in decades. And he had a very distinctive way of fighting." She looked at them both. "I knew who you both were the moment I saw you. I see a lot of your grandfather in the both of you. And lucky for you, Surya isn't attending the festivities because he tries very hard to hate and ignore anything that reminds him of his best friend."

Vishal opened his mouth to deny, but Vikram stopped him. "Are you going to say anything to Mr. Suryaprakash?" Vikram asked.

The woman looked at them both. "No. I'm just happy that your grandfather decided to put aside his ego and extend his friendship to Surya once again."

"What had happened to cause the rift between the two friends?" Vikram asked.

Lakshmi's face became somber. "Surya married the woman Vishwa was madly in love with."

Vikram and Vishal were taken aback with the piece of information.

"Surya didn't want to. But Bhanu had forced his hand and he had no choice." She looked at Vishal. "The Bhanu you know is a lot like her namesake, her grandmother. She can be rash at times, but she's a girl with a huge golden heart," she said.

Vishal had a look of disbelief.

"Bhanu and Sangeeta's parents died in a car accident," Lakshmi informed. "The oncoming truck driver was drunk at the time. So, Bhanu can't tolerate drunks."

Vishal was surprised, but he remained quiet.

"And Dinesh, the man whose hair and mustache Bhanu shaved off," she continued "He had gotten one of Bhanu's friends pregnant promising to marry her and then dumped her cruelly. That was the second girl he had gotten pregnant and cheated on so far."

"I see," said Vishal with a slight frown on his face.

"All those people she keeps meeting are the people who reach out to her for help. Sometimes, Geeta and I worry about her that in the quest to help others, she might get hurt one day. I hope you're there to protect her at that time."

Vishal's frown grew in size. "If you know who we are, you must also know our stay here is going to be temporary," he said. "We're here only to convince Mr. Suryaprakash to meet his childhood friend."

Lakshmi smiled. "I hope both of you succeed. Friendship like what Vishwa and Surya had is rare and precious." She headed to the door. "I have to go. Ask for me if any of you need something," she said before leaving.

As soon as they heard her walking out of the barn, Vishal shook his head. "Whoa, that was totally unexpected. You think anyone else knows who we are?"

"I don't believe so. Even if they do, they don't seem to want us gone."

Vishal shook his head. "I can't believe that Grandfather loved someone. And I'm not sure how I should feel towards Suryaprakash Gulati. He stole the woman Grandfather loved. That is totally against any friendship or brotherhood code."

"Well, apparently the woman whom Grandfather loved didn't love him back. And from what we just heard, Suryaprakash was forced by circumstances to marry the woman his friend loved. We shouldn't hold that against him. Especially when Grandfather doesn't want to hold any grudges towards his friend."

Vishal nodded. "True."

***

Vishal and his brother joined back the festivities later that evening. Unlike in the morning, Suryaprakash joined the events that night which were dedicated only to the classical events.

A makeshift stage was made in front of the temple where the cultural programs were to be held. The first program was a classical dance performance by Sangeeta and Bhanu Gulati.

Vikram and Vishal stood at a distance where they could see the programs while having enough privacy to talk.

"I hope we find enough time with Suryaprakash once everyone gets back to their routine," said Vishal while glancing at the stage. His eyes fell on Bhanu, and automatically anger rose up as he recalled her stupid stunt that morning. But he controlled his anger. Whatever Lakshmi had said about Bhanu might be true, but that didn't give her the right to put his life at risk.

He continued to watch the Gulati sisters move in graceful movements to the classical music. Grudgingly, he had to admit that Bhanu looked effortlessly beautiful and graceful in both traditional and western wear.

Not that I care or should even bother about that fact.

Vishal turned to Vikram to ask him about their important work-related meeting back home when he saw the expression on his brother's face. *What the fuck?*

Vikram's eyes were intent on the stage with a look that spoke volumes. His eyes were riveted on the older Gulati sister.

"Bloody hell, brother!" Vishal said with a slightly panic-laden voice.

"What?" Vikram asked, still not tearing away his eyes from the stage.

"Stop it right now!"

"Stop what?" Vikram asked in a distracted tone.

"Stop looking at Sangeeta like that, bro. You're making me nervous."

"Like what?"

"Like you're deciding how many children you'd have with her and whether to send those children to bloody Oxford or Cambridge."

"Don't be stupid."

"I'm not, but it's going to be extremely stupid and not to mention shit-full of complications if you fall for her and plan a future with her."

Vikram didn't reply. Vishal doubted whether Vikram even registered what they were discussing. He only continued to stare at Sangeeta like he was utterly captivated.

Great. Hundreds of women tried and failed to get the attention of Vikram Saaho over the years, and even their mother was sick and tired of showing Vikram hundreds of pictures of eligible brides, and now this.

Vishal's older brother was more or less devouring Sangeeta Gulati with his eyes, making it obvious that he wanted her and was badly smitten by her.

Keeping their promise was definitely going to come with a shit ton of complications!

CHAPTER SEVENTEEN

Bhanu was pacing about in her room.

For what seemed to be the hundredth time, she almost stepped out of her room, but quickly turned back.

Bhanu knew she owed Vishal an apology even though he was still a thorn in her side.

Yes, he was blackmailing her saying he would tell the truth of what she had done to Dinesh. And yes, he was being way too bossy and showing way too much attitude even though *he* was working for *her*. But did that warrant putting him in such danger? No.

Dammit!

Emitting a deep sigh, and before she changed her mind yet again, she stepped out of her room. She went down the stairs and to the back of the house and into the barn where his room was located at the back. She pushed the door open and strode inside and then tripped over something.

She almost broke her nose on the floor, but something or rather someone grabbed her shirt from behind, stopping her fall.

She heard the familiar yet annoying rich, masculine laughter. "I always had women falling for me. But no one literally fell for me like you, Princess."

Immediately, irritation flared like a tidal wave. "Very funny," she retorted as she pushed his hands away and straightened. "I came here to—" She broke off when she took in the sight in front of her.

Vishal was wearing shorts. And nothing else. He must have been exercising, because his tanned, muscular body was glistening with sweat. And the faint smell of masculine sweat combined with the smell of musky cologne was oddly intriguing.

Almost helplessly and curiously, her eyes explored him further. She hadn't noticed much about him until then because she had ignored him most of the time. But now, she did.

He had broad, wide shoulders and a chest with well-defined muscular arms. But his waist and hips were narrow. He was hairy, but not too much.

A golden chain was glistening within the smattering of his chest hair and she spotted a medium-size tattoo on his chest. The tattoo utterly drew her curiosity even further.

Her eyes immediately searched all over, looking for other possible tattoos. There were none. But the rest of him was equally fascinating. He had strong, powerful and hair-roughened thighs and legs.

Bhanu's brows drew together in a frown when her eyes fell on the large bulge in his shorts. It seemed to grow in size.

The next moment, her cheeks were on fire when she realized why. Her eyes flew up to his.

Vishal's eyes were glittering darkly as he stared back at her. "Have you had your fill? Or do you want me to shed my shorts so you can inspect my body some more?"

"I-I..."

He raised an eyebrow when she couldn't get any words out. And then, a slow, smug smile formed on his face. "It's okay, Princess," he drawled. "I understand. It must be my raw magnetism and constant presence this last week. No woman with normal instincts can resist me."

His arrogance was outrageous!

"Go to hell!" she snapped. "I wish you had got beaten to a pulp!" She knew it was a silly and childish of her to say such a thing, especially considering she had come to apologize to him. But for the life of her, she couldn't think of a better thing to say or do. She was too embarrassed.

Turning away from him, she fled out of his room, her face still on fire.

She heard laughter from behind her. "Did you want me beaten to a pulp so you could play my nurse and ogle my bed-ridden form even more?" she heard him asking.

Bhanu wanted to snap back at his wisecrack, but she continued to run away as though the devil was after her.

God, maybe the devil is after me. Or why else would I gawk at the dimpled arrogant devil of all men like that?

Bhanu didn't know if she could face that infuriating man again. But she had no choice as he had to drive her to college again in a week when her college break was over. Hopefully, her grandfather will not compel her to take that blasted man as her bodyguard for too long.

***

Later that day, Vikram and Vishal were summoned by Suryaprakash.

Suryaprakash looked at them both with a smile. "All I've been hearing from people is how you both won the fight against at least a dozen men. Where did you learn how to fight like that?"

"We learned that in the city," Vikram replied. "It's called Krav Maga. One of our neighbors was an instructor and taught us during our childhood for free."

"I see. Well, I'm proud of you both."

"We heard you were very good at these fights yourself, sir," Vishal added. "And that you had participated in them for the longest time."

Suryaprakash went silent for a while. "I used to participate, but I wasn't the best. There was another man who always won the fights."

"Oh. Who? Maybe we can take some tips from him," said Vishal, knowing full well it was his grandfather.

Suryaprakash was silent again before he decided to reply. "He no longer lives in the village."

"Oh. That's unfortunate."

This time, Suryaprakash didn't reply. He simply nodded appearing to be lost in his thoughts. "I'll see you both later," he told before leaving the room.

Vishal sighed. "You think he's thinking of grandfather?" he asked.

"Yes." Vikram hoped that they were good memories.

CHAPTER EIGHTEEN

Two days after the Banni festival, things settled down and went back to normal in Srirampur.

Bhanu and Sangeeta were tending to the garden along with Lakshmi when they heard a woman's rude shouting.

"Where the hell is everyone!"

Bhanu recognized the voice. "Ugh!" she said with a grimace.

"Bhanu. Be nice," Sangeeta warned.

A middle-aged woman swept into the backyard with a haughty, outraged face. When she saw Bhanu and Sangeeta, the older woman frowned. "Why is there no one to receive us?" she demanded.

Bhanu stood up and dusted her muddy hands before smiling sweetly. "Maybe because, as usual you dropped in unannounced? Don't they have phones in the city?" she asked.

The older woman's eyes narrowed, and she was about to snap at Bhanu when Sangeeta intervened. "Hello, Uma Aunty," she greeted with a smile. "Varsha! What a surprise," she said to a younger woman who was hesitantly and meekly following her mother at a distance.

"Lakshmi," said Sangeeta. "Please tell Grandpa that Uma Aunty is here along with Varsha."

Lakshmi nodded and was about to leave when Uma Gulati stopped her. "While you are at it, have mine and Varsha's rooms cleaned and prepared. And do a good job this time and not a sloppy one like the last time. I don't want to see any cobwebs hanging from the ceiling. And the sheets better smell nice."

Bhanu clenched her teeth at her aunt's rude tone and orders directed at Lakshmi. Just because Uma Gulati was married to the oldest Gulati son, the woman felt the house and the people working in the house belonged to her. She also thought she had every right to bully or be rude as she wished.

If only Bhanu could give her aunt a piece of her mind. She caught Sangeeta's warning gaze before Sangeeta led their aunt and cousin inside.

71

Bhanu reluctantly followed. Only to witness Uma Gulati barking some more orders. This time at Kamala to bring them tea and snacks.

Soon, they sat down around the old, sturdy dining table which was at least a century old.

"So," said Uma Gulati with a mocking interested look. "What's going on in your lives? Anything exciting happening in this village?"

The tone and the way the older woman said 'this village' was synonymous with 'godforsaken place.'

"Yes," Sangeeta replied with a smile. "We just celebrated the Banni festival a few days ago. You, uncle, Dheeraj and Varsha should definitely join us the next time."

Bhanu huffed inside. Suryaprakash Gulati extended the invitation each year to his son and his family. But so far, the esteemed family were yet to honor them by visiting the ancestral home during the festival.

Uma Gulati laughed. "How quaint that at your age you still think having such celebrations is fun," she said.

Bhanu saw red. But Sangeeta's hand gently squeezed hers under the table warning Bhanu not to react.

Sangeeta continued to smile. "Yes. I guess I'm the type who'll always enjoy it regardless of my age," she said.

The older woman looked puzzled, as though she wasn't sure whether or not Sangeeta was really the type to be polite, even if the situation didn't warrant it.

"You know, my dear," Uma Gulati said. "I've always told you that being a doctor, you would make much more money in the city rather than being stuck here in this tiny village. And not to mention that a pretty girl like you would easily find someone in the city to marry again. Your grandfather is as usual being selfish, keeping you two girls with him as old-age security."

Bhanu was unable to keep quiet any longer, especially when the integrity of the person she loved the most was being questioned. "Grandpa is *not* forcing us to stay with him!" she erupted. "Geeta and I *want* to be with him."

The older woman simply looked amused at the outburst which infuriated Bhanu.

Drawing in a calming breath, Bhanu let out a slow, deliberate smile. "But maybe you are onto something, Uma Aunty," she said with a thoughtful look. "If you and uncle were to convince Grandpa to live his old age with his only son, then he might agree. If that happens, Sangeeta and I would be more than happy to move to the city as well. And that too, with you. Just like old times." Bhanu widened her smile.

A horrified look passed on Uma Gulati's face at the suggestion. "Uh... I always tell Dharam we should get his father to stay with us, but he tells me that his father won't like the city life and prefers to live in the village."

"Maybe so," Bhanu replied. "But you should throw in that suggestion to Grandpa during this visit. And maybe Grandpa, Geeta and I can come along with you when you return to the city." Bhanu turned to her sister. "Geeta, aren't you excited to live in the city once again?"

Sangeeta remained quiet while Uma Gulati sucked in a noisy breath.

"Let's not be too hasty," the older woman replied. "There must be quite a lot of pending work remaining here. And besides, Srirampur is a good place to spend during old age. Didn't Srirampur win the model village award this year, too?"

Before Bhanu or Sangeeta could answer, their grandfather did. "Yes. Srirampur won the model village award this year, too," he replied proudly joining them at the table. "How are you, Uma?" he asked with a warm smile.

They exchanged the usual pleasantries. "I'm as usual doing well, Papa," Uma Gulati said with a smile. "And you look very healthy and active, too. I keep telling Dharam he should retire early so we can move to Srirampur and lead an active, healthy life."

Bhanu couldn't again stomach the fake, affected persona of her aunt. Of course, the end game of the other woman was to milk the old man out of as much money as she could.

The fact that she or her husband barely visited the village—except once a year when she dropped in to collect the money gained from the crops—rubbed Bhanu the wrong way. Sangeeta had told Bhanu many times not to get worked up about something she couldn't change. But it still made Bhanu fume.

It wasn't like Dharam Gulati was a pauper. As a practicing doctor who ran a successful hospital in the city, he had quite a lot of money. Yet, each year, the amount of the 'rightful share' was always picked up promptly by his wife. And several not-so-subtle hints were dropped wanting to remodel the ancestral home to their liking. Couldn't they at least wait until Suryaprakash Gulati at least passed away before coming down on him like vultures to pick him apart?

Taking a deep breath, "Excuse me," said Bhanu and got away from the toxic woman.

Sangeeta had told Bhanu not to be too prejudiced against her aunt. But how can Bhanu not be? It wasn't like Bhanu formed an opinion on Uma Gulati based on the brief flying visits.

Nearly ten years ago, after the death of Sangeeta and Bhanu's parents in an accident, Bhanu and Sangeeta were sent to live with their uncle and his family. That one-year stay was pure hell for Bhanu and her sister. Especially for Sangeeta, although Sangeeta kept telling Bhanu she was okay most of the time.

Uma Gulati could not stomach that Sangeeta was far more intelligent than her son, Dheeraj. Despite having maids in their house, Sangeeta was made to work, so she wouldn't find enough time to prepare for her medical entrance test. Although Bhanu was young, she could sense the petty jealousy of her aunt towards her sister.

Bhanu had always argued and fought with her aunt, but when it came to a point where her uncle and aunt were considering sending Bhanu away to the village, Bhanu grudgingly kept her mouth shut.

Not because Bhanu wanted to stay with Uma Gulati, it was because Bhanu didn't want to be separated from her sister.

Despite everything, Sangeeta was the top ranker and got into the best medical school with a scholarship. Dheeraj could also get into the same medical school with the help of a huge donation. And thanks to Sangeeta, whose help he had taken to prepare for the entrance, he had at least gotten qualifying marks in the exam,.

After the medical college began, Sangeeta had shifted to a woman's hostel, taking Bhanu along with her. They had a tough time managing things on their own at their age, but they both at least had peace of mind. And when Sangeeta graduated from medical school, they both moved to the village to live with their grandfather whom they both loved madly.

Bhanu sighed as she recalled what she and Sangeeta had decided for their future. When their grandfather passes away—which hopefully wasn't for many, many years—she and Sangeeta would build a smaller home within the village. Sangeeta would continue to run her practice while Bhanu hopefully would work from home on small IT projects like building websites for various companies. Not the most challenging job, but it would do.

Bhanu sighed once again. Another envelope from yet another top university arrived for the Master's program. Based on the weight, Bhanu knew it was another acceptance letter. This would make it the fourth acceptance letter so far.

The courses and the opportunities those programs were very tempting. If only...

Shaking her head, Bhanu pushed the temptation out of her mind before heading to the kitchen to help Kamala.

CHAPTER NINETEEN

Vishal was heading to the main house towards the kitchen to grab some lunch when he almost ran into a woman.

"Excuse me," he said absentmindedly, his thoughts revolving around on a work-related problem.

There was a gasp. "It's you," he heard a woman say.

It took a couple of moments to push his current thoughts away and focus on the woman in front of him. Vishal frowned. He had never seen the woman before. She appeared to be in her early twenties and had similar features to Bhanu and Sangeeta.

"You're the man from the club!"

Vishal froze for a split second before asking, "What club?"

"The exclusive nightclub in the city." She told him the name of the club along with the address.

He put on a puzzled expression. "I haven't been there and neither have I heard of the place. You're mistaken. And if we've met before, I would have definitely remembered." He smiled at her, hoping she would let go of the topic and leave.

But her eyes widened as she stared at his smile and she blinked a few times before responding. "No. I'm pretty sure it was you. I recognize your dimples, too! My friends and I had a bet that night to see who would catch your attention. But none of us could talk to you or approach you because of your bodyguards."

Oh shit. This one seems too determined. He needed to play it safe, so he wouldn't ruin it for himself and Vikram.

He continued to smile. "I wish I was that man who caught your attention at the club. But unfortunately, I'm not. I work as a driver for the Gulatis. For Bhanu Gulati in particular."

The woman seemed taken aback. "A driver?"

"Yes."

She shook her head in denial. "No. It is you. I have pictures from that night, too. That man looked exactly like you." She looked at the mobile in her hand and began browsing frantically. Then she stopped and gave her phone to him.

He held it and looked at the phone. It was thankfully a grainy picture of him from a distance. He shrugged, continuing to smile. "I can't see much of this man since it's dark. But I do agree, we seem to have somewhat similar features from a distance."

A cloud of doubt passed the woman's eyes before falling on his hands and they widened again. She held his hand and pulled it closer. "A golden Rolex! I saw this glinting on your hand that night too." Her eyes fell towards their feet. Luckily, the shoes he was wearing were comfortable sports shoes unlike the high-end Italian boots that he had worn that night. "How do you explain a Rolex?" she asked.

Before he could reply, a familiar feminine voice replied instead of him.

"It's a cheap knock-off," Bhanu said in a cool tone.

The woman holding his hand jumped back at the interruption, letting his hand go.

"What are you guys doing?" Bhanu asked with a cool look.

Vishal hadn't seen Bhanu for the last two days. After she had more or less devoured him with her eyes, she had avoided him completely.

That should have made him happy. But unfortunately it didn't. It only made him think of the bratty woman even more, especially during the nights.

"I just asked you both what the hell is happening here?" Bhanu snapped. This time her tone wasn't cold. There was annoyance.

Good.

"Talking," he drawled out. "I was talking to..." Damn, he didn't know the woman's name since he hadn't bothered to ask.

"Varsha," the woman answered. "I'm Bhanu's cousin. My father and her father were brothers. My mother and I are here for two days to spend some time with Grandfather."

"He doesn't need to know your entire history," Bhanu said irritably. "Come with me. Your room must be prepared."

"But I... he..." Before her cousin could complete the sentence, Bhanu dragged her away. And when they were about to go into the house, Bhanu turned and threw him another pissed-off look.

Now, what is she so pissed off about?

***

Bhanu was annoyed and she didn't know why. *Liar. You know why. You didn't like them touching.*

Ugh! She needed her subconscious to shut up, so her logical brain could begin thinking and act accordingly.

"This is your room," Bhanu practically threw her cousin in the guest room next to her bedroom. "Now, don't step out of the house unless you need something. And even then, call for me. Don't talk to anyone."

Varsha looked confused. "Why? You're acting as though that man is a criminal. In fact, I suspect he's actually a rich—"

"He's a criminal. A possible murderer, in fact."

"What!" Now there was genuine shock and fear in her cousin's eyes.

"Yes. In his drunken state, he actually confessed to someone yesterday that he killed his girlfriend and is hiding in the village along with his brother. Grandpa doesn't know because I didn't want him worried. I have sent information to the police and they are investigating. Until things are safe, don't mention this to anyone."

"Oh my God! Killed? Are you sure?"

"Yes. The police might arrive at anytime."

"But... but... he is so hot. How can he be jealous of another man? And which girl in their right might would want to cheat on him or even look at another guy?"

Bhanu almost rolled her eyes. God save her from stupidity.

You aren't that far off when it comes to him. You think he's hot, too.

Again, Bhanu wanted her inner voice to shut up.

"Exactly why he must have gone into a rage," Bhanu continued to say. "Such men are too egotistical. Stay away until the police get here!"

"Okay," Varsha said in a reluctant tone.

Bhanu turned on the television set. "I'll call you when it's lunch time. Watch TV or call me if you want to go out." With that, she stepped out of the room.

She almost ran into another person, but she stopped at the last moment by placing her hands in the front. Her palms met with hard muscles on a masculine chest.

She raised her head only to see the most annoying smirk on Vishal's face. "Murderer, huh?" he asked. "I didn't know that you had such good imagination, Princess."

Bhanu's face felt like it caught on fire. "What are you doing here and listening in like a thief?" she snapped.

He held a phone out. "Came here to return your cousin's phone."

Bhanu realized her hands were still on his chest. Vishal raised an eyebrow, his smirk widening.

With her face feeling even hotter, Bhanu snatched her hands back and stepped away from him as though he had a contagious disease.

Then she pulled the phone from his hand, "I'll return it. Stay away from my cousin!" she warned.

She turned the other way, trying to get as far away from him as she could, when she heard his amused and annoying laughter.

***

Vikram was checking the latest accounts when a sweet feminine voice interrupted him.

"Vikram?"

He closed the laptop screen to give all of his attention to the woman who had lately has been occupying most of his thoughts.

Sangeeta smiled warmly at him. "This is my aunt, Uma Gulati. Aunty, this is Vikram, our new accountant. He can help to let you know how much money you'd get for half of our yield and also help you transfer that amount to your bank account."

Vikram tore his eyes away from Sangeeta to look at the older woman accompanying her.

"What happened to Ranjan?" the older woman asked with a frown.

Vikram knew she was referring to the old accountant.

"He had to leave because of family problems," Sangeeta replied.

The older woman didn't look happy at all. And Vikram knew why.

Over the last two weeks, he had gotten familiar with all the Gulati household accounts. He had noticed that each year, around the same time, a huge chunk of money was transferred to a bank account. The chunk that was transferred was way more than half the share of the crop sale. Vikram guessed that the previous accountant must have helped and was probably bribed by the older woman to get a bigger share.

"Why wasn't I consulted before hiring a new accountant?" the older woman demanded.

"Grandpa made the decision and we are happy with Vikram's work. He's very good at what he does."

The older woman still didn't look appeased. With a huff, she stormed out, leaving Sangeeta behind.

"Sorry about that," Sangeeta said softly. "She arrived this morning and must be still tired."

Vikram highly doubted it. But he knew Sangeeta was the type to give everyone the benefit of the doubt.

"It's okay," he said while slowly taking in her appearance.

Sangeeta was wearing a simple dark-colored dress that she seemed to favor over light-colored ones. A small smudge of dirt on her forehead indicated she had been gardening like she usually did during the mornings.

Vikram realized that while he was taking in her appearance, she was doing the same with him. There was silence while they stared at each other. But it wasn't an awkward silence.

Vikram was reminded of Vishal's observation of how Vikram stared at Sangeeta in a certain way. He knew it was true. He was quite fascinated by Sangeeta. And the object of his fascination and admiration didn't seem to mind either. Sangeeta always had a warm smile for him, which turned a little shy when they locked eyes on each other and she caught him staring, which was most of the time.

A jarring voice interrupted their moment.

"*Geeta!*" Uma Gulati's shout was heard from somewhere in the house.

Sangeeta jumped and then she slowly blinked before another shy smile covered her lips. "I'll see you later," she softly said before leaving the room.

Vikram sighed as he continued to stare at the spot Sangeeta last stood.

Something was building between him and Sangeeta. It was subtle, but it was definitely there. Even though he was ready to acknowledge it, he didn't know if he was going to do anything about it.

CHAPTER TWENTY

A day and night of torture filled with incessant boasting continued from the annoying visitor.

"My Varsha is getting so many alliances. Most of the prospective grooms work for multinational corporations abroad. Those grooms' parents are all after us to consider Varsha getting married right away, but we are waiting until she finishes her final year. By the end of this year, we plan for her to be married."

Sangeeta was in the clinic. So it was just Bhanu, her grandfather and the older woman. Bhanu stayed only because she couldn't afford to leave her grandfather at the scheming woman's mercy.

"Varsha's wedding will be the next happy occasion," her grandfather said with a smile. "The entire village will celebrate it grandly."

"Personally, I would prefer that, too," Uma Gulati said. It was followed by a fake regretful smile. "But you know how the youngsters are these days. They all want a foreign-destination wedding."

Suryaprakash's face fell a little. "If not the wedding, we need to host a celebratory event here."

"Of course."

Suryaprakash glanced at Bhanu. "You know, Bhanu will be completing her final year at the same time as Varsha. Let me know if there are good alliances for her, too. NRI ones should be okay, too."

Before Uma Gulati could respond, or Bhanu could protest, Kailash burst into the room. "Sir, you are wanted urgently!"

Suryaprakash frowned. "I'm coming." He then looked at his daughter-in-law. "If I'm not back on time, have a safe journey, Uma," he said.

As soon as the older man left, Uma Gulati looked at Bhanu with a wide, satisfied smile. "You know, I can throw some of Varsha's rejected alliances your way," she said. "But I don't think any man would even want to be with someone mouthy and abrasive like you. Especially the rich NRIs. They'll either want a compliant wife or a skilled mistress. You are neither, my girl."

Bhanu tried not to show any visible reaction or explode like how she wanted to.

"But don't worry," the older woman continued. "We'll sponsor yours and your sister's airline tickets and hotel stay for Varsha's wedding. It may be the only time you little frogs will ever get to step out of your little well."

With that statement and a short, satisfied laugh, Uma Gulati left the room to pack her bags.

***

Vishal was talking to Vikram outside the barn when they heard a commotion from outside. They went to the front of the house to investigate and saw a large group of men standing in front of the house with anxious looks.

Before Vishal could enquire, Suryaprakash came out hurriedly from the house.

"What happened?" Suryaprakash asked.

"Sir! Goons from the city have entered your fields, and they are building a fence around the land that is along the highway!"

"What! How dare they!" He looked at Vikram. "Let's go quickly."

"I'll come along, too," said Vishal.

He drove the car while Suryaprakash gave the directions to the lands that were running along the highway.

As soon as he pulled the car over under a large tree, he saw at least half a dozen vehicles parked close by. They got out of the car and went towards where around twenty muscled men stood around waiting while several workers installed a barbed fence.

A few people from the villager gathered around, but were watching the sight helplessly.

Suryaprakash went towards a man sitting on a chair under a large umbrella. He was shouting instructions to the men asking them to hurry up.

"What's going on here?" Suryaprakash demanded. "Didn't I already refuse to sell you my land?"

The man on the chair looked at Suryaprakash. A wide, obnoxious smile covered his face. "Come on, Mr. Gulati. I've asked you nicely so many times over the last year. You already knew how powerful and land-hungry my boss is. You should've listened when you had the chance."

"This land belongs to my granddaughters upon my passing! I'm not letting you or anyone snatch away their birthright." Suryaprakash strode towards the men installing the fence. "Stop this right now and leave my land. Or I'm going to call the police and have you all arrested."

There was laughter from the obnoxious man and his goons. "The police won't do anything, Mr. Gulati. In fact, I know most of them. Nice fellas."

Suryaprakash looked agitated. "You may be able to bribe a few, but you can't bribe them all." He took out his phone and dialed a number. As soon as it was answered, he spoke to the person on the other end. "Basi Kumar and his people are on my land right now. I want you to come here and warn them away."

Slowly, Suryaprakash's face changed and he looked angry and disappointed. "What do you mean they have papers that show the land is theirs!" he shouted into the phone. "This land has been in my family for generations." Whatever the other person spoke only made Suryaprakash more upset. "How can you say you are sorry! I will—" He broke off with a frown, probably realizing that the other person ended the call.

In his agitation, Suryaprakash strode towards a man installing the fence and tried to pull him away. But a goon interfered and shoved Suryaprakash back.

Vishal was pissed that the goon shoved an old man. He strode to the goon and punched the goon in the face until the other man staggered. But another goon began to close in. When that goon was about to hit Vishal, Vikram stopped the oncoming blow and shoved the goon back.

But soon, the rest of the goons began to close in.

"Stop," said Suryaprakash in a shaky tone. "Vikram. Vishal. Please, stop. Let's leave. This isn't worth it."

When Vishal continued to glare at the goons, an obnoxious voice warned Vishal. "Listen to the old man, buddy. Don't try to be the hero. Leave when you have the chance."

"Vishal. Vikram," Suryaprakash pleaded. "Please, let's leave."

At Suryaprakash's plea, Vishal and Vikram reluctantly turned away from the goons and followed Suryaprakash to the car.

As they drove away, Suryaprakash appeared devastated. "This land is the only thing I have to give my granddaughters when I pass away. And Basi Kumar is right. There is nothing I can do to protect my own land. The man who seized the property is a powerful politician."

Vishal and Vikram remained silent.

As soon as they reached the Gulati house, Suryaprakash disappeared into his room.

***

Vishal was pacing in the barn. "We should go confront that obnoxious bastard and warn him to leave the land alone," he said with an angry frown.

"No. That's risky as it might reveal our identities too soon."

"Then maybe we can have Tanuj and Pooja make arrangements to hire a lot of goons and have the ones occupying the Gulati lands thrown out."

"No. That'll raise a lot of questions, too. I think I have a plan."

"What plan?"

"Investments. I don't think grandfather would mind anymore if we were to make large investments in India."

Vishal immediately understood his brother's plan and slowly smiled. "I think that's a great idea. I'll call Dad tonight and make the necessary calls."

Vikram nodded.

CHAPTER TWENTY-ONE

The next morning Vikram was woken up by the sounds of excitement. When he came out of his room, he saw some familiar faces of the villagers. Suryaprakash was talking to them.

"Sir, they all left!" one of the men said with excitement. "The cowards must have gotten scared of our threats yesterday and ran away overnight. They even removed the fence they had installed!"

Suryaprakash had a look of disbelief and kept shaking his head. "This is so unbelievable. It's truly a miracle. The politician called me personally a few minutes ago to apologize to me for the misunderstanding. He also informed me that he is going to make a large donation to our village so that we don't have any hard feelings towards him."

While Suryaprakash and the villagers continued to talk excitedly, Vikram slipped away to meet with Vishal.

"How much?" he asked.

Vishal smiled while getting ready to resume his driver duties. "The Saaho Corporation has promised the state government to invest rupees two thousand crores in the next two years. In turn, they would require certain favors with no questions asked. Last night was the first favor."

"Good."

"One of us has to go for that meeting in the city tomorrow to sign the contracts in person."

"You should go," Vikram advised. "I don't think Suryaprakash would mind if you take a day's break."

Vishal nodded. "All right. I'll let Suryaprakash know this evening. I'll talk to Dad in a few hours and let him know as well."

***

Bhanu pressed on the car horn impatiently.

Where the hell is the dratted man!

She felt irritable and angry. She had been awake all night since she couldn't sleep. Her aunt's petty words had gotten under her skin.

The pathetic picture that her aunt had painted of Bhanu and Sangeeta being just the poor relatives, who would have to depend on their rich relatives' handouts to experience the world, rubbed Bhanu the wrong way.

Bhanu knew she shouldn't allow a jealous woman's words get to her. But she couldn't seem to help it. With a deep sigh, she tried to push her thoughts away once again. She hoped that college and classes would help distract her.

Where the hell was Vishal? He should have been ready and waiting in the car by the time she finished her breakfast and stepped out.

Bhanu was tempted to get into the car and leave. If only the annoying man hadn't confiscated the car keys.

It was really too much that he was still getting away with so many things all because she didn't want to see disappointment on her grandfather's face.

And worse, he had caught her in the act of ogling him and later lying about him to her cousin.

At first, she was embarrassed, but later she decided there was nothing to be embarrassed about. She had made it a point that during the last few days, each time she saw him, her chin was raised and she met his eyes boldly, daring him to embarrass her.

But nothing seemed to faze the blasted man. He only looked amused at her challenging stare.

With another impatient sigh, Bhanu pressed on the horn again.

"What's the hurry, Princess?" an amused voice asked.

Bhanu swung around to glare at Vishal. "I've been waiting for a very long time. Didn't I ask you to be ready by seven thirty?"

He raised an eyebrow. "You did. And so I am," he replied.

She looked at her watch. It was only seven twenty-five. Dammit! She raised her chin again. "My bad. Let's go."

There was a flash of surprise on his face at her almost apology.

Ignoring him, Bhanu sat quietly as he started the car and drove them out of the gates. She didn't turn on the music like she usually did.

When they passed the village limits, he broke the silence. "What's with all this silent brooding?" he asked.

Bhanu turned her head to snap *'Mind your business!'* but she stopped herself.

She stared at him instead. She could only see his profile. He was wearing sunglasses that looked expensive. But she knew they must be another cheap knockoff that he must have purchased in the city.

A few moments passed. "What's going on in that pretty head of yours, Princess? You're making me nervous." He spoke to her while keeping his eyes on the road.

His words triggered something inside her. "You think I'm pretty?" she asked.

He threw her a brief look. "Now you're just fishing for compliments. Don't you have enough admirers stalking you to sing praises of your beauty and what not?"

She didn't reply. "Who is the richest man in the city where you lived?" she asked instead.

He raised an eyebrow at the complete change in topic. "Not sure. But there are a lot of rich men in the city. The current market is hot enough that people are getting richer by the day—"

"Do they travel? To outside countries?"

He frowned. "Yes."

"Hmm. Do you think any of them would consider having me as their mistress?"

He looked shocked at her question. "What?" He turned to look at her face as though to confirm whether or not she was joking.

She looked at him without flinching or embarrassment. "I'm planning an affair with a rich man. The richest I can find."

He didn't laugh or mock her like she thought he would.

"Why?" he asked in a disbelieving tone.

"Why not?" she demanded.

He ran his eyes over her intently. His gaze moved from the top of her head to her feet and then back again. "Because usually women like to think that being a wife is much more respectable than being a rich man's mistress. Especially most naive virgins who stay in a village don't have ambitions of becoming someone's mistress."

"I'm not a naive virgin!" She felt her cheeks heat at the lie. "And I don't ever want to get married. I can't leave my grandfather or sister. I just want to be a rich and powerful man's mistress for a while."

"Again, why?"

"To prove a point to someone."

He shook his head. "Your reasoning and your goal are quite silly, Princess. Not to mention self-destructive." His tone sounded brutally honest.

"I don't care!" she snapped defensively. "Just tell me all the names of the richest guys in the city that you know of. Looks are not that important. Neither is age. He should be kind and possibly malleable, allowing me to do whatever I want and live wherever I want."

He shook his head at her bizarre and brazen request. "It's not that easy being a mistress of a rich man. Men, however pliable on the outside, would just use you and throw you out after they had their fill. It takes real skill to keep a man enchanted. So stop trying to hatch a plan that would do more harm to you than help you."

It was ironic that a man was warning her against the predatory nature of men. She knew he was right. But she was determined to pursue her path. She would somehow bag a rich, powerful man and be his mistress.

CHAPTER TWENTY-TWO

Vikram was seated outside the Gulati house chatting with Suryaprakash. Vishal had just come in and joined them. Vishal had asked for permission to travel to the city for a day for which Suryaprakash agreed.

"I'm not against people choosing to live in the cities or abroad," Suryaprakash said with a smile. "Wherever you live, it's important that you are close to nature and give back to it as much as you can."

"But I do hope you liked Srirampur and would return," the older man told Vishal with a smile.

"I definitely will, sir. I'll be back the day after tomorrow morning," Vishal replied.

"Good." Suryaprakash looked at Vikram. "You can join your brother, too, if you want, Vikram."

"That's not needed, sir. It's just a small official thing. Vishal can get it sorted in a day and return soon."

The older man nodded.

Now that the crop cutting and Banni festival were over, Vikram began to spend more time with Suryaprakash.

It was quite interesting that when it came to personalities, Suryaprakash was very different from Vikram's grandfather. Vishwanath Saaho was rigid in his rules and discipline, and way too practical ever to make decisions based purely on emotions. On the other hand, Suryaprakash was still disciplined, but most of his decisions were based on emotions.

While Vishwanath Saaho was feared and respected, Suryaprakash was well-liked and respected. It was interesting that two men who were so different in their ideologies had a close friendship and bond for many years.

"Have you ever lived in the city, Mr. Gulati?" Vishal asked.

"No. I visit my older son and his family once in a while, and I just stay for a day or two. But when my younger son was alive, I used to stay at his place for a week or so."

"What about abroad?" Vikram asked. "Have you gone there for visiting?"

There was silence. The older man seemed to get lost in his thoughts. Then shaking his head slightly, Suryaprakash smiled. "No. I haven't. And I don't plan to either."

"You should, Mr. Gulati," said Vikram. "My previous employer in the city often went on trips abroad. He was an organic and sustainable farming enthusiast. He mentioned that they have good conferences where you can meet like-minded people and learn about the latest agricultural technology and techniques."

"I see. Where are these conferences held?"

"The one my employer attended often was in London."

The smile dropped from Suryaprakash's face. "I'll never go there," he said in a vehement tone.

Vikram or Vishal remained silent.

Suryaprakash shook his head with a sigh. "Sorry for my outburst," he said quietly. "It's just that London reminds me of a person I don't want ever to see in my life."

"I'm sorry about that. A relative?"

"No. A friend." There was a pause. "He used to be my best friend until he chose to cut off all ties."

"If he was your best friend, he must be of similar age as you. Don't you think time heals everything and people should forgive one another at later stages in their lives?" Vishal asked.

Vikram knew Vishal was pushing it slightly by being too personal, but they had to broach the subject sooner than later.

Suryaprakash wasn't offended. He looked thoughtful. And then he sighed. "I'm usually forgiving in nature. But I can't forgive him for what he did."

"What did he do?" Vishal asked.

There was another long silence. Just when Vikram and Vishal thought there wouldn't be an answer, Suryaprakash replied. "He didn't fulfill the wish of my dying wife."

With those words, the older man got up. "Excuse me," he said before disappearing inside.

Vishal sighed. "This is taking forever. What were Bhanumati Gulati's last wishes? And why did our grandfather choose to ignore it?"

"I think only one of the two friends can answer that," Vikram replied. "Our job is to first ensure Suryaprakash gets to the state of mind to agree to meet grandfather."

"Yup."

"So for tomorrow's meeting," Vikram began to advise. "Make sure they keep the news of our investments confidential until we tell them that it's okay to release it to the public."

"Tanuj has already told them. But I'll reiterate it to them. Some of the politicians are apparently too eager to brag that it's because of their hard work that they got the Saaho Group to invest in their city."

Vikram nodded. "All right. Call me from there if you need anything."

"Yup. I'll hit the bed early tonight. The bus is going to arrive quite early in the morning and Tanuj will wait in the neighboring village with a chopper."

Vikram didn't answer. He spotted Sangeeta who had just come out of the clinic and was chatting with a group of women.

It was almost six thirty, way past the clinic closing time, and yet there was no fatigue or tiredness on Sangeeta's face. She smiled, laughed and continued to chat as the women spoke to her.

As though she could sense his gaze, she looked in his direction. When she caught him staring at her, her smile widened.

Vikram's heartbeat sped up and he was once again stunned by his reaction.

Why did he always react to her that way?

Yes, she was beautiful. But over the years, he had been in the company of many beautiful women. Then why was he reacting like an infatuated teenage boy to this particular beautiful woman?

It must be her smile. It was warm, mischievous and infectious—all at the same time. It hit him like a punch.

"Stop it, bro!" Vishal's amused voice ordered.

Vikram half-turned towards Vishal. "What?"

"You want her." The statement sounded like an accusation.

Vikram gave all of his attention to his brother. "I don't know what you mean," Vikram replied in a cool tone.

"If you don't hide your feelings, the entire Gulati household, including Suryaprakash, will know how you feel about Sangeeta."

"I don't have any feelings for anyone."

Vishal watched him keenly. "That's good. Because *I* want Sangeeta."

Blind rage hit him. "You can't have her," he commanded before he could think or stop himself. Then immediately, he realized he had been set up.

Vishal slowly grinned. "Well, well. For someone who doesn't have any feeling towards her, you sure do sound quite possessive."

Vikram gave his younger brother a thunderous frown.

Vishal laughed. "I know you are supposed to be the mature one among us, big bro" he said. "But don't do anything stupid while I'm gone."

Vikram didn't bother commenting on that statement. "Call me when you reach the city tomorrow," he said instead.

After Vishal went back to his room, Vikram's gaze automatically fell towards the clinic. Sangeeta was still talking to her patients.

Vishal was right. He did feel possessive about Sangeeta. Even though he had no claim on her whatsoever, the thought of his brother or for that matter *any* other man wanting her, made him feel like breaking something. Which was very strange because even while he was in a few relationships before, he had never felt possessive about any of those women.

"Vikram?"

Through the haze of his thoughts, Vikram realized someone was calling him. He turned to see Suryaprakash standing near the doorway with a quizzical look on his face.

Vikram realized that the older man must have asked him something while Vikram was busy staring at his granddaughter. "Yes, sir?"

"I was telling you that I'd like to stay home tomorrow."

"Sure. Not a problem, sir."

Vikram knew he was in trouble when he realized that he was waiting in anticipation to be able to join Sangeeta for lunch the next day.

CHAPTER TWENTY-THREE

Early next morning, Vishal heaved a sigh of relief when he stepped out of a surprisingly crowded bus.

He had been quite tempted to pull a stunt similar to the last time by asking Tanuj to book all the tickets of the bus. But he knew it might raise doubts, especially if the ticket collector and the driver of the bus turned out to be the same as before.

As soon as he stepped out, he was received by Tanuj and two personal hired bodyguards. Vishal waved away their offer to carry his luggage bag and followed Tanuj as the other man led him to a waiting helicopter.

"The meeting is confirmed at one o'clock, Vishal. Here's the list of politicians and bureaucrats we'd be meeting." Tanuj continued to provide details.

A couple of hours later, the helicopter landed on top of a luxury seven-star hotel where Vishal would be staying for the day.

"What time would you like me to reserve a table for lunch?" Tanuj asked. "There are three restaurants below that are quite good."

"Just order room service. Something simple."

As Vishal freshened up in the penthouse suite of his hotel room, his eyes fell on the sights outside. The tall skyscrapers and the mad rush of the traffic seemed worlds apart. After spending nearly two weeks in Srirampur and living a simple life, Vishal found it a bit strange to return to his world even if it were for a brief time.

But he wouldn't find time to relax as he had to go over the papers and contracts with Tanuj and a legal team before the meeting.

He wished he could grab a brief shut-eye. He had barely slept the entire night. His usual calls were done well before midnight. But he still couldn't sleep because he was thinking of a certain bratty woman and their strange conversation the previous morning.

What the hell did she mean by she wanted to be a mistress to a rich man? And who did she want to prove a point? And what point?

He was thinking in those lines feeling alternately annoyed, strangely angry and also frustrated.

And much later, when it was finally dawn, he got off the bed in self-disgust.

Why do you care what she wants to do or says? his logical brain had demanded. *Stop thinking of unnecessary things and focus on what is needed.*

He then firmly decided to follow those instructions. Push Bhanu Gulati out of his mind.

***

The meeting started right after lunch. It was held in one of the conference rooms of the hotel.

"Mr. Saaho, we are truly honored that the Saaho Group has decided to make investments in our city. But if I may ask, why haven't you invested in India before?"

Vishal shrugged at the man asking the question. "No particular reason. We didn't think the timing was right. But now that we know there's a huge potential in the current market scenario here, we wanted to go ahead."

It was the truth. For many years, Vishal, Vikram and their father had tried to convince their grandfather to make investments in India. But Vishwanath Saaho had been adamant not to. Vishal now knew why.

It was almost evening by the time the meeting was almost done and the final paperwork was signed off. Vishal would be heading back to Srirampur during the early hours the next day. He didn't have the patience to take a bus, so the helicopter would be dropping him in a relatively close spot by the fields around three in the morning.

Vishal got up from the chair and shook hands. "All right, gentlemen, my team will continue to work on these projects," he said.

He went out of the conference room and stood in front of the lifts that would take him to his suite upstairs. Tanuj and the bodyguards were present with him.

While they were waiting, the sound of clicking heels sounded in the otherwise quiet lobby.

Vishal turned to see a woman wearing high heels walking towards them.

"Mr. Saaho, I have something important to say to you. Can we have some privacy?" she asked.

Vishal recognized the woman. She was present in the meeting, but Vishal had no idea what her role or designation was.

He gave Tanuj a discreet look after which Tanuj and the bodyguards quietly disappeared.

Vishal looked at the woman. "How can I help you, Miss...?"

"Shika," she replied with a sultry smile. "My father is the current IT minister." She stated the name of the man who was an integral part of the meeting. "When he told me that the Saaho Group was interested to invest in our state and that Vishal Saaho was coming in person for the meeting, I wanted to join."

The way the woman said his name out loud, Vishal immediately knew what she wanted. It was definitely not to discuss work or investments.

"Now that you're done with all of your meetings, can I join you upstairs?" she asked further confirming his conclusions. "I heard there's a breathtaking view from the penthouse suite. I've never been to this hotel before."

Under normal circumstances, Vishal would have flashed a smile and escorted her upstairs where they would spend a hot and pleasurable night together. But something niggled at him.

"I had a long day and I have to leave quite early tomorrow, Shika," he said.

Her sultry smile didn't waver at his polite brush-off. It became wider. "Don't worry, I can be quick," she said, pulling him close by his collar before whispering the next words. "I also don't expect you to make any promises when we're done. In fact, I promise to blow your mind with pleasure." She then ran her lips on the side of his neck.

It had been a while since he spent a night with a woman. And the beautiful woman in front of him who came with no strings attached was exactly his type. Then why was he hesitating?

Maybe because unlike before, he found the overly done perfect makeup a bit off-putting. The short, tight dress that showed off feminine assets was also not doing a thing for his body. And most of all, the overly pleasing smile that was plastered on her face killed his interest completely.

Bloody hell!

"I'm sorry, Shika," he said while gently pushing away her arms from around his neck. "I have an important call to attend to in a few minutes." With that, he turned away and pressed the button to the lifts.

"But—" Before she could complete her sentence, one of the lift doors opened letting out a small group of people.

"Goodbye, Shika. All the best to you," he said, stepping into the empty lift.

As soon as the doors closed, he swiped the suite key card and pressed the button to the top-most floor where his suite was located.

He kept staring at the lit buttons on the lift panel.

He had just realized something important. He realized that he wanted a woman who wore minimal makeup, wore simple, understated clothing, and worst of it all, he craved a woman who couldn't care less of wanting to please him. He wanted someone who constantly challenged him.

Fuck! Bloody, bloody fuck!

What his mind had just described was Bhanu Gulati.

CHAPTER TWENTY-FOUR

Bhanu felt restless. It was a Saturday and she didn't have to rush to get ready for college. She woke up at the usual time in the morning and helped Lakshmi and Geeta get started on the weekend house cleaning. Later, after having breakfast, she helped pluck the vegetables from the garden.

All the while, Bhanu's thoughts kept going to one person. Vishal.

It felt odd not to have him around the previous day. Upon her grandfather's insistence, she had taken Ravi—one of the workers from the rice mill—along with her to the college. It was not the same as having Vishal.

For one thing, Ravi was way too deferential and sat in the back seat while she drove. Ravi barely talked to her during the drive, much less crack any smart-ass remarks or argue with her.

Why are you missing smartass remarks directed at you, anyway?

And not just the smartass remarks, she even missed seeing the damn dimples.

You really need help.

Bhanu's musings were interrupted when she vaguely heard someone calling her name and shaking her slightly.

"Bhanu!"

Bhanu slowly blinked and looked at Sangeeta who was watching her with a quizzical expression.

"Yes?" Bhanu asked.

Sangeeta looked amused. "Never mind. We're done plucking the vegetables. Just add the ones you collected to the basket so Kamala can begin cooking."

Bhanu looked down and noticed she barely had any. Just a couple of tomatoes. Sangeeta and Lakshmi had filled their baskets.

"Sorry. Something's on my mind," she said.

Sangeeta smiled. "Obviously."

Bhanu looked at Lakshmi. "Have you fed the puppies yet?"

"Not yet."

"I'll do it," she offered.

A few minutes later, Bhanu entered the barn and poured some warm milk into a large bowl for the puppies. After their mother, a stray, was bitten by a snake, Bhanu had rescued the puppies and brought them home a couple of months ago.

While the puppies drank their milk, her eyes kept going to the closed door at the back of the barn.

Did he return?

Maybe he decided to stay back in the city.

Good riddance!

Even as she thought that she would be better off without him, a part of her felt oddly disappointed at the thought of him never returning.

Bhanu was distracted when all the puppies finished their meal and then ran out of the barn to play around the house. Except for one. This one was tugging at her shoes, determined to play with her.

***

Vishal woke up to the sound of feminine giggles.

"That tickles."

"You're so naughty."

More giggles.

Vishal was irritated. He had gotten back to the Gulati house during the early hours and he had barely slept in the last forty-eight hours. And now, someone was having a secret fling outside his room. He closed his eyes, determined to shut out the disturbance.

"I know you like it when I touch you like this. Don't you?"

Vishal's eyes popped open all of a sudden when he finally recognized the voice through his sleep-fogged brain.

How bloody dare she!

Intense fury filled him, and he threw the bed sheet aside before going to the door and kicking it open. He stormed out, ready to kill the man she was with. But as soon as he saw her, he stopped short.

Bhanu was on her knees. And she was playing with a puppy that was wiggling in her arms and trying to lick her face. She looked at him in surprise, maybe because his face must be still reflecting his fury.

"What are you doing here!" he snapped.

She slowly and gently let the puppy out of her arms which promptly skipped away. "I live here. You know, because this is *my* house and you work for *me*."

The damn brat never missed a chance to remind him of that fact.

"Well, this part of the house is assigned to me. While I'm here, stay away from this place." He knew he was being ridiculous. But the irrational rage and jealousy thinking she was with another man was making him lash out at her. And his realization from the previous day of wanting her added to the fury.

She didn't care about the rage on his face. In fact, she seemed pretty pissed, too.

"I'll go where I want and when I want," she taunted with a raised chin. "And right now, I want to go inside *my* barn room. Who's going to stop me?"

She stood up and began to stride towards his room.

He stopped her. He wrapped his arm around her waist and pulled her towards him until her body crashed into his.

She let out a shocked gasp which he ignored.

The soft curves and the familiar smell of her subtly perfumed soap drove him crazy. He wanted to drag her inside his room and keep her there, until the ache she created in his body, and the confusion she created in his mind were all gone.

As soon as that thought passed in his mind, he sobered up immediately. *What the hell are you doing!*

He immediately let go of her.

He expected her to slap him or at least scream for help all the while threatening him dire consequences. And she was more than justified for grabbing her like that.

But she was watching him. Not with an offended look but with a curious look. That bloody look heated his blood. "What?" he snapped once again.

"What's that on your neck? Is that... lipstick?"

He frowned, and he got reminded of the previous evening when a woman had made a pass at him at the hotel.

"Did you kiss a woman?" Bhanu asked when he remained quiet while continuing to glower at her.

The reminder also made him pissed that he rejected the advances of that beautiful, available woman because he only wanted the brat standing in front of him.

"Have you slept with many women?" she prodded further.

"None of your business," he snapped.

Instead of being offended at his rude tone, her curious eyes seemed to bore holes in him. "I noticed that sometimes... you look at me as though... I don't know... as though you... uh... want to kiss me."

Kiss was a tame word compared to what he wanted to do to her right then. "That's because you have a hot little body," he said in an irritable tone. He was hoping to goad her into anger so that she would storm out before he said or did anything stupid.

She wasn't angry and that damn speculative look continued to stay on her face.

"What's going in that head of yours?" His tone came out moody. His brain must have stopped working because of lack of sleep and because the woman in front of him was making him crazy with lust and annoyance.

She continued to watch him. The way she was slowly moving her eyes over his body began to arouse his body. Since he was only in his shorts, she could see what effect her staring was having on him. This was the second time she had caught him this way.

And instead of being embarrassed or outraged, she raised her head to look him in his eyes. "Kiss me," she said all of a sudden.

"What?" He was more than stunned by her request. Surely, his mind was hallucinating due to his lack of sleep and unrequited lust for the woman in front of him.

"I said kiss me," she repeated.

"No!" The woman was going to drive him insane.

Her eyes flashed and she had a challenging look on her face. "Come on. I know you were thinking of kissing me just now. You also think I'm hot. I'm giving you permission to kiss me."

He sucked in a breath. "It's my day off, so leave me in peace. Get back into the house right now!"

She raised her eyebrow at his order. "Fine. If you don't want to, I'll find someone else to kiss." She turned and began to walk away.

An irrational anger filled him again. He chased behind her and wrapped his arm around her waist and pulled her close until her body was plastered against his. This time, he held the back of her head before crashing his mouth on top of hers.

He captured her lips and shoved his tongue between them and into her mouth. His body exploded in heat.

His tongue lay siege as he madly and desperately explored every nook and corner inside her mouth. Her sweet moans and passionate movements against him drove him insane. He pulled her even more closer and continued to devour her. He did to her mouth what he wanted to do to her body. His tongue mated with hers.

When he was shaking with need, and was about to explode, he pulled his mouth away, intending to put a stop to the craziness. But he froze when his eyes fell on her face.

Instead of being overcome with passion like him, she looked disgusted. She struggled and immediately broke free of his hold and took a few steps away from him, making him realize that what he had assumed as passionate movements of hers was actually her trying to escape his arms.

She vigorously began to wipe her lips with the back of her hand. "Ugh! Kissing is disgusting," she said with a grimace.

Despite his body screaming in arousal, he felt offended. "No. It isn't." At least kissing *him* wasn't.

"It is! Those things you just did to me with your tongue... eww... I don't know how women even bear it, let alone want it voluntarily."

Vishal scowled. Women from his past had labeled him as the best kisser. His body was screaming in agony as he was painfully aroused by their passionate kiss. And the damn woman found it disgusting?

Through his lust-filled mind, he slowly realized that despite her bold facade, Bhanu was quite innocent. This particular kiss was most likely her first ever kiss. And his loss of control because of wanting her for too long had made him kiss her like she was an experienced partner.

With a determined look, he pulled her back into his arms. She struggled again trying to escape, but seeing his determined expression, her struggles stopped. She looked curious. "What are you doing?" she asked.

He didn't reply. He pulled her even closer and held her captive by holding the back of her head and wrapping an arm around her waist. And then, he slowly bent his head towards her. She continued to watch him curiously.

This time, he started slow. He slowly brushed his lips against her slightly reddened ones. She kept her lips tightly shut, making it obvious she didn't want his tongue inside her mouth once again.

He didn't force his way in and kissed her with several small and soft kisses, joining their lips together.

Within a few moments, her eyes closed and her breath began to come out in soft pants like his. And then, she slowly began to kiss him back.

A few moments later, he sucked in her plump bottom lip and applied slight pressure on it with his teeth, making her gasp aloud and open her mouth. He then began exploring the rim of her lips with his tongue.

After much heavy breathing and some more kissing, he slowly slipped his tongue inside her mouth. This time, she was more than receptive. She actively participated by widening and offering her mouth to him.

She moaned softly as his tongue touched hers. She even tried to mimic him by rubbing her tongue against his.

He growled low in his throat while she whimpered softly when he increased the intensity of their kiss.

When his need grew too unbearable and before he completely lost his control, he pulled his mouth away from hers and stared at her face.

Her eyes were still closed and she was breathing hard and fast like him.

Slowly, she blinked her heavy-lidded eyes open. "Wow," she said softly.

He continued to watch her brightly, flushed face. "Now do you like kissing?" he asked.

"Yes."

"Good," he said even though the lesson made the ache in his body ten times worse.

Reluctantly he dropped his arms from around her to put some distance between them.

Meantime, she continued to watch him with an odd look on her face.

"What?" he asked. His tone wasn't as harsh as before.

"Teach me."

He frowned, not following her.

"Teach me how to kiss," she said. "And uh... and maybe later some other things that follow after a kiss."

"No!" he more or less growled. His body was hanging on a thin thread, and this request was pushing him to the edge.

But his tone didn't seem to deter her. She shook her head as though she was shaking away her daze. And when she looked at him again, she had the determined, stubborn look.

"Why not?" she asked. "If I'm to be a rich man's mistress, I need to learn the skill of seduction. Since you seemed to be experienced and good at it, you can teach me."

Bloody hell!

"Stop going after that stupid idea," he ordered. "You're not cut out to be anyone's mistress. Rich or otherwise."

She raised her chin. "It's not a stupid idea. I am going to be a rich man's mistress. If you don't help me, I'll find one of the guys from my college to help me."

"Not on my watch!" he snapped. "I'll break those guys' knees and every bone in their body, if they ever come close to you, let alone touch you."

She didn't seem perturbed by his violent threats. "Hahh. You can't guard me inside my campus," she returned. "But I'd rather you teach me. Because those other fools will want to marry me at the end. I don't want to marry anyone ever."

He scowled as his sleep-deprived brain threw in visuals of her with any one of the fools from her college who always followed her like love-sick puppies. One of those clumsy morons getting the chance to kiss and touch the fiery, passionate woman in front of him made him see red.

Like hell, I'd allow that!

He dragged her close once again and swept her off her feet. She gasped in surprise as he held her in his arms. But slowly a smug smile covered her pretty face when she realized she had won.

It pissed him off and aroused him at the same time.

He carried her inside his room and kicked the door shut, determined to kiss the hell out her.

CHAPTER TWENTY-FIVE

Vikram was seated in the small office room along with Suryaprakash. They were going over the weekly accounts.

"And from your rice mills, last month your income was—" He broke off when a soft feminine voice called out. He looked up from the accounts and saw Sangeeta standing near the doorway.

She was dressed in an elegant sari with simple jewellery. Her eyes fell on Vikram, and when she caught his intense gaze watching her, she hurriedly looked away with her cheeks reddening slightly.

"Grandpa…" she said. "I'm going to Neerja's wedding."

"Oh good. Give my blessings to them."

"I will." She looked unusually hesitant. "Grandpa… Kailash took the day off today."

"Oh. So are you going with Ravi, then?"

"Ravi also took the day off."

Suryaprakash frowned. "That's so irresponsible of them. I'll have a word with them both when they return."

"It's okay, Grandpa. They work hard for us and are allowed to take some breaks. Anyway, I was wondering if Vikram is free and can join me for the wedding. He can meet people from the village."

"That's a great idea." Suryaprakash looked at Vikram. "We can catch up on the accounts tomorrow, too, Vikram. Go with Sangeeta to the wedding. You'll get to socialize with people from Srirampur."

Vikram nodded. He closed the laptop and stacked up the accounts printouts before standing up. "I'll see you later, sir," he told Suryaprakash. And then, he looked at Sangeeta. "Let's go," he told her softly.

***

It was an hour's drive to the wedding during which they chatted casually like they did during their lunches.

When they reached the location, Sangeeta was greeted warmly by the bride's family and led inside.

Vikram noticed that everyone made it a point to greet and briefly chat with Sangeeta. And in return, Sangeeta had a ready smile and spoke to each and every one of them. She even tried to include him in most of the conversations.

"How do you like living in Srirampur so far?" an old man asked Vikram.

"It's good."

"So will you settle down here, then?"

"I'm considering it, yes."

"That's good." The old man smiled. "We have many eligible women at a marriageable age. So you don't have to go outside to look for a bride. In fact, weddings are great places to look for prospective brides. Let me introduce you to a few."

"That's not needed, sir. But thank you for the offer. Please excuse me." Vikram stepped away and headed to the refreshments table.

Sangeeta joined him. She was smiling widely, looking thoroughly amused. "You should have taken up the offer to meet some eligible brides," she teased.

"You could have rescued me," he said with a smile.

She laughed. "I was having too much fun looking at your reactions to put a stop to the conversation."

He shook his head, smiling.

"But don't worry," she said. "I promise to rescue you the next time. And believe me, you are going to be sought after quite a lot during such occasions."

Sangeeta was right. Over the next few hours, Vikram was cornered by at least five other older men and women who seemed hell-bent on setting him up with someone or the other. But luckily, as promised, Sangeeta stayed by his side to rescue him.

By the time they left the wedding, it was late afternoon.

Vikram enjoyed the pleasant drive with seemingly endless green fields on both sides of the road.

"That must be quite a movie," he said while keeping his eyes on the road. "That both Kailash and Ravi decided to go and watch it on a working day."

"Yes, it is," Sangeeta replied. "I heard it is—" She broke off and looked at him. "I didn't tell Grandpa or you that they went to watch a movie. How did you—" She broke off again when he turned to look at her with a small smile.

A blush covered her face and she shifted uncomfortably. "They did go to a movie," she said in a defensive tone. But they both knew who had paid and sent the two men away to watch a movie on that particular day.

Vikram found her blushing and attempting to cover up her lie to be entirely charming. Continuing to smile, he looked back at the road.

He was about to say that he was flattered by the fact that she had gone through all that trouble just to spend some time with him. But suddenly, the car jerked. He held the steering firmly while the car continued to jerk and also make some sputtering noises.

"What's happening?" Sangeeta asked in slightly panicked tone.

Vikram frowned. "I'm not sure." He slowed down and pulled the car over to the side of the road. "I'll be right back," he said before getting out of the car and going to the front.

He opened the hood to see if he could determine the problem. There was heat radiating from the engine.

The sound of the car door opening and shutting indicated that Sangeeta had stepped out as well.

She stood next to him in front of the car. "What happened?" she asked.

"We'll need to add more coolant," he said. And considering it was an old car, he knew there probably were other things that had to be checked as well.

"The mechanic shop is nearby," she said. "Let me call them and you can give them the details." She dialed a number and handed him her phone.

A man answered and Vikram spoke to him, letting the mechanic know what to bring along before he gets to the car.

When he was done instructing, he ended the call before and handed Sangeeta the phone. "They said they'll be here in a few minutes," he said.

Sangeeta nodded. While she took back her phone, the small purse she was holding slipped and fell on the ground. Immediately, he bent to pick it up. She had the same intention.

Their heads bumped together lightly and his hand covered hers over the small purse strap.

Slowly, they stood up straight while he continued to hold her small, soft hand in his. She didn't pull her hand away from his gentle grip.

He saw her blushing again, and she lowered her eyes while a shy smile formed on her lips.

A few days ago, Vikram had made peace with the fact that he not only found Sangeeta beautiful, he was also extremely attracted to her. Sangeeta had a sweet and simple aura that further added to his attraction. He always felt a strong need to take her into his arms and kiss away her worries and cherish her. And the fact that even she liked him was only making things harder for him to resist her.

But he knew he had to.

With a great amount of effort, Vikram let go of Sangeeta's hand and stepped away. "Let's wait under the shaded tree while the mechanic gets here," he said softly.

***

Sangeeta stood under the tree while watching Vikram talking to the mechanic. Vikram's sleeves were rolled back, and there was grease on his arms as he helped with the repair.

Why can't I keep my eyes off of him? she wondered.

Something about the silent, dignified man pulled her towards him. She had known Vikram for only a month or so. And during that time, even while she was having the busiest of days, her thoughts often ran over to him.

Was it because of Vikram's intense stares whenever they came across each other? She wondered what went through Vikram's mind while he watched her. Not that she remotely minded him watching her. In fact, she immensely enjoyed them.

She liked him. Even her grandfather couldn't stop singing praises to tell her how lucky it was for them to have men like Vikram and Vishal working for them. Especially Vikram. Her grandfather spent most of his day with Vikram, and besides the finances, she had heard them talking about other topics too. She joined them sometimes whenever she was free. And she especially looked forward to and thoroughly enjoyed the times when she and Vikram had their lunch together.

Sangeeta didn't know whether it was right or wrong, or whether she wanted to control her feelings, but the fact remained that she was beginning to fall for Vikram.

For the first time in her life, she felt the feelings of longing for another person. She knew that she not only liked Vikram, but she had a strange longing to always be close to him and talk to him.

Those feelings had initially made her feel guilty, because she had never felt that way towards her late husband. Maybe because she and Sirish had never really had a chance to get to know each other well or interact that closely on a personal level. She only knew Sirish as a fellow doctor in the village.

When her grandfather had asked her to marry Sirish, she never thought twice before agreeing. It had made sense because she and Sirish had similar goals and outlook in life.

When Sirish passed away, she had felt sad and mourned his loss. But it was more as an empathetic fellow human rather than a devastated loved one.

She knew it would be different when it comes to Vikram. He had the power to crush her heart if he wanted to. So, did she want to take chances with him to hand her heart over?

She didn't know the answer to her current dilemma.

Pushing her thoughts away, she continued to watch Vikram.

He finished talking to the mechanic. Wiping his hands on the small rag offered to him, he came towards her.

"It'll take some time for them to fix the car," he said. "I've already instructed them on what needs to be done. Let's go home."

"How?" she asked.

"They offered us to use their bike. They'll drop the car off at your house and take their bike."

Sangeeta nodded. She followed Vikram as he led her to the bike. He opened the seat and placed the rag inside before taking out a helmet.

He handed it to her.

"You should wear it," she said. "You are the one driving the bike."

"Wear it, Sangeeta," he said in a firm tone.

She was about to argue that he should be the one wearing it, but before she could speak, he put the helmet on top of her head and secured the strap under chin.

"Let's go," he said.

Because of her attire, Sangeeta had to sit sideways. And since there wasn't enough purchase or anything she could hold on to, she sat gingerly while trying to balance properly.

"Hold on to me tightly and don't let go," she heard him say softly before he kick-started the bike

With her heart racing, and reading way too much into his words, she tentatively placed her hand on his shoulder.

She could feel the hard muscles of his shoulders and could smell the clean and pleasant smell of his cologne. Sucking in a deeper breath, she savored the sensations.

Soon they were heading home.

As they went past the fields that looked beautiful in the evening setting sun, she slowly came to a conclusion.

Yes, she was willing to take chances to hand her heart over to Vikram.

CHAPTER TWENTY-SIX

"My lips hurt!" Bhanu realized that her voice sounded whiny, but she couldn't help it. The sun was setting in the sky and Vishal was half-lying on top of her. They didn't have much privacy near the house, so they had to sneak out into the open fields. They were behind a large haystack in one of the fields. They had just finished a heavy session of kissing and pulled away to draw in much-needed air into their lungs.

Vishal grinned. "My poor baby," he said, rubbing his thumb slowly and gently against her swollen lips.

Bhanu stared at his dimples. Her entire body tingled as he continued to rub his thumb on her bottom lip. Over the past two days, they had been kissing nonstop as though they were determined to discover all the ways their mouths could fit together. It was thrilling, but she felt too restless wanting to know and also do so much more.

"When are you going to teach me other things apart from kissing?" she demanded. Her hands crept back into his hair, already preparing to pull his lips on top of hers.

Vishal's eyes flashed fire before he let out a slow, heated smile. "Kissing is quite a vast subject, Princess," he drawled. "And there are lots and lots of other ways to kiss." His smile grew wicked. "And in many interesting places, too," he added.

Bhanu felt a rush of heat and excitement taking over. Show me!" she commanded.

And he did.

***

"Bhanu?"

Bhanu looked up from her textbook. She saw Sangeeta standing near the bedroom doorway.

"Busy?"

Bhanu put the book aside. "No. Come in."

Sangeeta smiled as she came in and sat on the bed next to Bhanu.

"It's been a while since we spoke for more than a few minutes," said Sangeeta. "I wanted to check to see if everything is fine."

"Everything is fine. The finals are starting soon, so I'm a little busy." Bhanu fought her blush as she recalled the real reason of why she was coming home late each day. The face of a dimpled, arrogant devil with a wicked smile and mouth flashed in her mind.

Bhanu desperately hoped that her extremely observant sister wouldn't notice her blush and lie. Luckily Sangeeta didn't.

"Don't worry about your finals," Sangeeta said with a smile. "I know you'll do very well and be the topper this year, too."

Bhanu smiled with a sigh. "I hope so, too."

"So, have you decided where you'll be studying next?" Sangeeta asked.

Bhanu hesitated. She knew her sister wouldn't like what she had planned. But she couldn't hide it for long. "I've applied for jobs that are close to Srirampur. They have good positions—"

"Bhanu!" Sangeeta looked disappointed.

Bhanu felt her stomach sink seeing that look on her sister's face.

"You have acceptances from the top universities in the world! And that too with scholarship offers! I told you so many times not to have second thoughts. Grandpa and I will be fine!"

"Whether or not I pursue my higher studies will not really matter, Geeta. Eventually, I'll have to get a job."

Her sister wasn't buying it. "You know that's not true, Bhanu. Yes, you're good enough to succeed anywhere, but don't throw away a golden chance because of a misguided attempt of family duty."

You did it, too. Bhanu wanted to say those words out loud to her sister, but she stopped herself. Because she knew it would only lead to an argument which they have had many times. An argument with no end.

So instead of arguing, she said, "I'll think about it."

Sangeeta didn't look entirely happy, but she at least no longer looked disappointed. "All right," she said. "So, how are your friends doing?" she asked Bhanu.

Bhanu told her. As usual, she regaled some funny or interesting incidents that happened in the college.

Sangeeta smiled and laughed as she listened. But then, soon a yawn escaped her. "Excuse me," she said with a sleepy smile. "I guess I need to hit the bed. Let's chat tomorrow."

Bhanu knew that her sister got really tired on the days of the free-clinic where she barely even had the time to grab lunch.

"Goodnight, little sis," said Sangeeta as she got up from the bed.

Bhanu looked at her sister's tired face. "Don't wake up early tomorrow, Geeta. I'll help Lakshmi with the gardening and collect the eggs."

"It's okay," said Sangeeta. "I'll be fine with a good night's sleep." Leaning forward, she kissed her younger sister's cheek. "Good night."

Bhanu stared at the door even after Sangeeta left.

She knew her plan wasn't perfect. But she was still determined to go ahead with it. She would get a job where she could work for a rich man as his personal assistant or something. Anything that would eventually lead her to be that man's mistress.

Hopefully, before next year, when Uma Gulati sent tickets to attend her daughter's wedding, Bhanu would be able to throw them back in her aunt's face saying that she can pay for her family's tickets and accomodation.

And hopefully, Bhanu would be able to take her sister and grandfather to many and much-needed vacations in style, and buy them things that they wanted rather than buy just things that they absolutely needed.

She was determined to spoil her sister and grandfather rotten giving them everything their hearts desired.

But of course, she would have to keep the fact that she was a rich man's mistress a secret. Knowing that she willingly sold her body to someone for materialistic purposes would simply break Sangeeta and Grandpa's hearts.

But what if Grandpa has a heart attack if he ever found out?

No! Don't think about it!

Bhanu took a deep breath, trying to push away the morbid thoughts from her mind. She let out a noisy exhale when her stomach continued to churn with worry and conflicted feelings.

Then suddenly it came to her. She knew what or rather *who* could release all of the tensions in her mind and body and fill her with mind-blowing pleasure instead.

. Slowly, she got down her bed. And with a determined look, she slipped out of her bedroom.

She then opened the back door softly and slipped out of the house. As she entered the barn and padded softly inside towards the room at the back, she recalled some of the things she had been doing with Vishal over the last week.

Things that the dimpled, arrogant devil did to her were quite shocking and dirty. But they were too exciting and entirely addicting.

All the places—and they were numerous—where he had kissed her began to tingle. Bhanu's heart thumped harder in anticipation.

If having an affair was exciting like this, then being a rich man's mistress isn't going to be a chore.

Even as she thought that, something niggled inside her, saying that maybe it was just this particular man who could make her feel that way.

Bhanu firmly pushed those doubts away.

CHAPTER TWENTY-SEVEN

It was close to midnight and Vishal had just finished all of his work calls. He was lying on the narrow cot with arms folded behind his head and staring at the barn ceiling.

He wasn't sleepy. He felt entirely too restless.

Like in the recent days, most of his thoughts revolved around a woman—an uptight, snooty and beautiful woman who constantly challenged him.

Of course, the moment he pulled her into his arms, she was no longer uptight or snooty. She was simply hot and beautiful while still managing to challenge him.

He recalled her moans and wild movements as he pleasured her every way he could. She pulled him closer and gasped out her release which sounded like music to his ears.

It was getting more and more difficult to control himself when he was with her. It was a miracle that he didn't just take her completely in the past few days. Even though his entire body hurt and demanded that he complete the act, the logical part of his brain stopped him.

He knew he shouldn't.

Vishal sighed. He closed his eyes trying to make his overactive brain to relax and push the thoughts of Bhanu away.

He still couldn't. But a small noise coming from the outside managed to distract him.

He heard soft footsteps approaching his room within the barn. Moments later, the door to his room opened, and the object of his thoughts came inside.

His eyes took in the thin and long nightwear of hers which was illuminated by the soft moonlight coming through the window.

"It's midnight," he said.

She shrugged an elegant shoulder. "I know."

"Then what are you doing here, Princess? You are supposed to be asleep."

She didn't reply immediately. She came closer until she stood right next to his bed.

He heard her take in a deep breath before she spoke.

"I want to make love," she said. "Go all the way. And I want to be the one driving it."

His already aroused body roared into life at her words. "No."

At his firm refusal, she frowned. "But, if you don't let me touch you or pleasure you or even have proper sex with me, how else am I to learn how to pleasure a man and be a good mistress?"

His brain stopped listening to what she said beyond the first few phrases. Touch. Pleasure. Sex. Those were the only words his brain processed. He groaned inside while she eyed his mostly bare body. Bare aroused body.

He was certain this woman was going to be the death of him someday.

He wanted her. He had long accepted that fact. During the last few days when they had kissed for the first time and done other things, he kept excusing his behavior telling himself that any red-blooded man would take up the offer that was laid out to him.

She was a beautiful woman who was full of fire and passion. What actually put him off guard was the fact that despite their rough start, even she was equally and strongly attracted to him.

He knew he could somehow control *his* desires, but he had no idea how to control *hers*.

But he had to try.

"I shouldn't have touched you in the first place," he said. "We went too far. Consider the lessons over. Now go back to your room, Princess. Make sure to lock your bedroom door." Or he might end up breaking into her room and demanding that she deliver on the promise her eyes and her words offered.

She didn't reply. The expression on her face shifted and she now had a stubborn look before she sat on the bed next to him.

Vishal groaned internally again. *I hope to hell I'm strong enough to withstand the onslaught of a curious, determined virgin.*

It turned out that he couldn't. At least not this particular curious, determined virgin.

The bed was too narrow. So, even as she sat gingerly on the corner of his bed, she was touching him. Soon, she bent towards him until she was half-lying on top of him.

She then began to kiss him the way he had taught her during the last few days.

This time, he groaned out loud in pleasure even as he cursed himself for teaching her or even touching her in the first place.

His hands automatically held her hips. Whether it was to pull her closer or to push her away, he didn't know. On some level, he knew he should stop her. But soon the logical part of his brain disappeared and his body had a mind of its own. And it craved the woman in his arms.

She sucked in his bottom lip before running her soft palms against his bare chest. When she bit his lip and moved her hands lower, he gave up the fight.

He tightened the grip on her hips before sweeping her underneath him on the narrow cot.

"That's it! I'm making you mine," he growled.

***

If Bhanu weren't floating in deep and intense sensations, she would have been snapping at the arrogant devil, telling him that *she* was the one who had wanted to drive their lovemaking before he took over. But she was enjoying this too much to protest.

She let out a gasp when he sucked her nipple into his hot mouth. As usual, she couldn't recall how or when he had gotten rid of her clothes. And this time, he had even gotten rid of his clothes.

Every sensation felt magnified because she could feel his hair-roughened skin along with his hard muscles wherever their bodies touched each other.

Moaning softly, she arched towards him and clutched his dark hair before pulling him even closer. But he seemed impatient to linger at her breasts for too long. His hot mouth moved lower, making her breath came out in gasps.

She knew what was coming, because he had done this to her many times in the last few days. But still, she could never get used to it or get enough of it.

With a few moments, his mouth tortured her with pleasure until her head was thrashing on his pillow. She turned her head and tried to muffle her pleasured cries by biting into his pillow.

She was so lost in sensations, floating in them so much that she only vaguely felt him widening her legs further and moving in between them.

She then felt his heavy weight settle on top of her.

She could hear his harsh breaths. Something thick and hard poked her sensitive area causing more tingles to erupt and making her shiver in arousal. Then suddenly there was a blinding, sharp pain as something huge entered deep into her core.

Her eyes flew open. Vishal was holding her tightly with his face buried in the crook of her neck. She could feel his hot breaths as he groaned and panted while his body remained completely still on top of hers.

She didn't like it. She didn't like it at all. It hurt.

She felt very disappointed that sex would be like this. Especially sex with him. So far, everything he had done to her was pleasurable and exciting. Except for the actual sex. But since she had demanded it and had already come this far, she decided to tolerate it. She closed her eyes and waited for him to finish.

But he didn't move or finish the act. His heavy weight held her motionless under him.

She felt him slowly moving his head away from her neck.

"Are you okay?" he rasped.

She shut her eyes tightly and didn't respond, hoping it would be over soon.

"Bhanu?"

He waited for a few more moments. "Open your eyes and look at me," he ordered when he realized she wasn't going to respond.

Bhanu didn't want to respond. But knowing him, the arrogant devil would pry her eyelids open to have his way. So she opened her eyes and glared at him.

She found him staring at her intently with an intense possessive look that caused a small pleasurable fluttering in her stomach.

"You're trying to kill me!" she accused in a furious whisper.

A small smile covered his face. "I know it hurts, Princess," he said. He gently brushed her hair away from her forehead and flushed cheeks to look at her better. "I heard it's supposed to hurt the first time for women, but you won't die." Slowly his smile grew, flashing his dimples. "Although, I'll make sure you experience a little death before I'm done with you," he vowed.

With that intriguing statement, he pulled out of her a little and thrust in again. She gasped clutching onto him by digging her nails into his shoulders. The pain was still there, but it wasn't as searing or intense as before.

He continued to thrust, making her want to buck and throw him off her to free herself from his invasion. But something in her mind that was thrilled with the idea of being this close to him stopped her from pushing him away.

All thoughts vanished when his mouth covered hers in a demanding kiss. Heat spread through her body, and it especially radiated from where they were joined together. His large, rough hands stroked her heavy breasts, and then her stomach before he held her hips. He joined them more and more deeply, again and again.

She lay pinned under him while her world shrank to the man on top of her.

Their hearts pounded within their chests as he continued to take her. And since she couldn't twist away or move much, she let herself only feel. Slowly, the pain became tolerable. And soon, she even began to crave his thrusts which were rough yet oddly hypnotic.

She moved along with him while he continued to invade her body and drew out pleasure.

He grunted, he groaned. And in between kisses, he whispered against her ear and mouth. Tender words, sex words and rough, dirty words she was now used to hearing and enjoyed listening to from him.

Her body came alive once again. Soon, she became hyperaware of him as she clung to him. The corded muscles of his body strained under her fingertips as he moved in relentless strokes. And then, it came—her release. It washed through her like a huge tidal wave, sucking her completely in.

Vaguely, she heard him roar his release into her neck before his huge body began shaking and trembling on top of hers.

She tried hard to open her eyes, but nothing could stop the deep, content blackness that completely took over her.

CHAPTER TWENTY-EIGHT

"Now you both seem like one of us, Vikram and Vishal," Suryaprakash said with a smile.

It was the planting season, and the entire Gulati household was in the rice paddy fields. Except for Suryaprakash, the rest of the household were ankle deep in wet, muddy soil while planting the rice saplings.

"Grandpa, if only they had dressed the part, too!" Sangeeta said with a laugh.

Vikram smiled at her. She was right. He and his brother hadn't planned on volunteering for the planting. But when Sangeeta got into the muddy soil and helped with the plantings, he couldn't take his eyes off of her. She was laughing and even singing folk songs along with the other village women while having so much fun.

She had caught him staring and teased him saying if he planted a few saplings, then he would pass through the rites of being a true farmer and villager at heart.

And so, rolling up his sleeves, and stepping out of his footwear, he stepped into the mud along with the rest of the workers.

"You youngsters continue with the planting," said Suryaprakash. "I'll check the rest of the lands." He walked away using his walking stick.

Over two months had passed since Vikram had arrived at Srirampur with Vishal. So far, they had made good progress. Suryaprakash Gulati liked both of them and spent each day talking to them. The older man trusted them and considered them to be a part of his household. Vikram only hoped that he could breach the subject with the older man as soon as possible.

"Bro," Vishal's voice interrupted. "If anyone were to take our pictures right now, they would make a fortune selling them," Vishal murmured in a tone only Vikram could hear.

Vikram smiled because it was true.

Unlike Vikram, Vishal had taken it up as a challenge and was planting the saplings rapidly. He was competing with the rest of the workers.

"Vishal, you missed a few spots." Bhanu Gulati pointed at the gaps where more saplings could be planted. "I've told you that it's more important to do a thorough job than just getting the job done."

Vishal straightened to look at her. "At times, it's better to get the job done as fast as you can, Miss Gulati," he drawled. "And then we can always go back for the second round for doing a slower, thorough job."

Vikram frowned. There was a decided undertone of sexual innuendo in what Vishal had just said. But the younger Gulati sister didn't seem upset or angry. She looked amused.

Before he could tell Vishal to cut it out, Vikram's phone began to ring. Wiping his muddy hands on his clean shirt, he pulled out the phone. He saw his father's number flashing on the screen.

"Excuse me," he said and stepped out of the wet, muddy soil.

He walked to a distance where he had enough privacy before he could answer the call.

"Dad? Is everything all right?" he asked.

"Yes."

"How is Grandfather?"

"He's doing better, son. But he wants you and Vishal to come and visit him for a day."

"Vishal and I are just beginning to earn the trust of Suryaprakash. If we leave right now, he might think we are returning to the city because we don't like village life."

His father sighed. "I know, son. Maybe if not both of you, at least you come. If Papa talks to you in person and listens to how his friend is doing, he might feel much better."

"And besides, your Mum misses you both," his father added. "Even with your jet-setting lifestyle, both of you made it a point to drop by once a week. It's been nearly a month now."

Vikram knew his father was right. He and Vishal had made it a point to spend time with their mother at least once every week or two. "Tell her I'll be in London tomorrow, Dad."

Vikram went in search for Suryaprakash. He saw him standing with Sangeeta who was giving him his daily dose of insulin.

Vikram went to them. "Sir. I just received a call from my father."

"Is everything all right?" the older man asked.

"Yes, sir. It's my grandfather. He has not been keeping well lately."

Suryaprakash nodded solemnly. "Yes. Family and loved ones should come first before anything else. You should go. We'll manage here for some days without you and your brother."

"Vishal will be here, sir. You can take his help if you need anything. I'll leave right now."

"Of course. Take your time and spend quality time with your family," said Suryaprakash. "All right, have a safe trip in case I don't get to see you by the time I return home." The older man patted on his back before he walked away.

Sangeeta remained.

"How many days will you be gone?" she asked after a few moments.

"I'll be back in a week."

She fell quiet. She began walking and he walked along with her.

"Will you really return?" she asked.

"Yes," he softly replied.

"Don't be too sure. Maybe once you go to the city and your family, you'll know what you've been missing."

They had walked quite a distance away from the fields. He stopped under a large shaded tree that offered them privacy from the rest of the people working around the fields.

"Sangeeta..." he said. Unable to control himself further, he gently nudged her face up with his fingers under her chin, until she looked at him.

Her eyes widened slightly in surprise and she visibly held her breath. He brushed a finger on her delicate cheeks, and unable to resist, he bent and brushed his mouth softly on her trembling lips.

He knew he was crossing the line as this was not the norm in the world she grew up in. But he really couldn't stop. Luckily, she didn't push him away. She gasped and closed her eyes.

He kissed her softly. Even the slightest of contact with her made a hard impact on him. But using all the discipline he could muster, he controlled himself from deepening the kiss. He knew that once he kissed her the way he wanted to, he would be powerless to stop the raging desire he felt for her. He would end up sweeping her up into his arms and making love to her right under this tree.

Soon, he promised himself. The moment he fulfilled the promise he made to his grandfather and revealed the truth of his identity to Sangeeta, nothing was going to stop him from making Sangeeta completely his.

He kissed her forehead. "I promise I'll be back. And I'll be back for you."

She looked at him as though she was memorizing his face. "I'll be waiting," she replied softly.

***

Vishal more or less dragged Bhanu behind him. The rest of the household was still in the fields planting when he had indicated to her that they should sneak away. He drove like a maniac to get them to their usual spot as soon as possible.

He threw her on the stack of hay and climbed on top of her.

"You are sweaty!" she said, wrinkling her little nose.

He grinned even as his hands rapidly pulled at her muddy clothes. "That's from my hard labor under the sun in the fields, Princess. Now give your man his due reward!"

Bhanu giggled. But as soon as his lips landed on her throat, it turned into a moan. He dragged his tongue along her neck tasting the salty tang and her sweet essence.

"I am sweating, too." She gasped breathlessly.

"Yes. And you're even hotter when you're wet and muddy like this."

He got rid of her top and put his mouth on her breast and sucked in a nipple. She clutched his hair and pulled him closer, her sweet moans driving him crazy.

He let go of her breast and sat up. At record speed, he got rid of their clothes and threw them in a heap at the corner. All the while, she ran her little tongue along his bicep and also his chest, tasting him and making him go even crazier.

He held the back of her long hair and looked her in the eyes. "I can't wait. I need you now." His voice came out as a growl.

She barely finished nodding when his mouth landed on her mouth. He swallowed her gasps while he pushed her legs apart. Soon, he joined them together.

She was more than ready and willing.

It was a raw, hurried coupling, and she was with him every step of the way, digging her nails into his back and pulling him closer as he drove into her again and again.

Even with the gentle breeze, they both turned even sweatier.

But it was over way too soon.

He couldn't control the onslaught of his release. He groaned into her neck as his release ripped through him. And luckily, she was in sync, muffling her pleasured cries on his shoulder.

Much later, when he was able, he slowly raised his body, so he wasn't crushing her. He looked at her face, feeling a little guilty for skipping the foreplay. Her eyes were closed, and she was still breathing hard and fast like him, but she had a content smile on her face.

He pushed her sweat-dampened hair away from her face and leaned over and kissed the tip of her nose where there was a smudge of mud. "You okay, Princess?"

She nodded and opened her eyes, her smile slowly widening. "Is this the part where you are going to come back for the second round and do a slower, thorough job?"

He burst out laughing. "Yup."

But before he could pull her close to kiss her thoroughly, his phone began to ring with the familiar ring tone. He groaned.

"What? Who is it?" Bhanu asked with a frown.

"My brother. Have to take this call, Princess. Stay where you are. I'll be right back." He rolled away from her and answered the phone. He walked away and stood at a distance for privacy.

"Vishal. Where are you?" his brother asked.

"Still in the fields. Why?"

"Dad called to say Grandfather wants to see us. I told him I'd go and you'll stay here. I'm leaving right now."

Vishal knew that if he left along with his brother to visit their grandfather, they might lose Suryaprakash's trust as the older man might think they were skipping because they didn't like the village life. So it made sense that just Vikram would fly to London. "Do you need help with the travel arrangements?" he asked.

"No. I've already sent a message to Pooja."

"Good. How long will you be gone?"

"At most a week."

"Okay. Call me when you get there."

Vishal ended the call and turned around to look at the beautiful, passionate and naked woman lying on the hay stack waiting for him with a smile.

He rapidly covered the distance between them using long strides. "All right, Princess. Time to fulfill my promise. Brace yourself, this is going to last a while."

"Hahh. That's what you say each time," she challenged.

Damn. She was right. But he was still determined.

CHAPTER TWENTY-NINE

Vikram had just stepped out from the flight when he saw his mother and father waiting for him by their car.

"I missed you, son." Vinita Saaho hugged Vikram.

"I missed you, too, Mum." He hugged her back and smiled at his father. "Dad."

"Welcome home, son." Rajesh Saaho patted his son on the back.

Vikram slid into the back of their limo and took the seat opposite to his parents. "Has Grandfather spoken anything else since?" he asked.

"He's able to speak some small words," his father said. "But with great effort."

Vikram's mother smiled. "You look tanned, son. Does your new job require you to stay outdoors a lot?"

Vikram returned the smile. "Not much. Vishal and I volunteered to plant rice samplings in the fields yesterday."

Vikram's father looked taken aback, but his mother looked thrilled. "That sounds like so much fun! I've always wanted to settle in a village somewhere in India."

"I didn't know that," Vikram said softly.

"Well, your grandfather hated India. And your dad was a workaholic until you kids grew up. So I always dreamed of a quiet, simple life while staying close to nature."

Vikram nodded. If anyone were to tell him a few months ago that he would enjoy living in a small rural village, he would have thought that person to be beyond stupid. He thrived on a fast-paced, challenging life.

But now, after having seen the simple way of living, he understood the charm in it.

Vikram looked outside the car through the tinted windows. The view of the London city with the crowded streets filled with cars was all too familiar, yet it seemed so far off from the place he had been staying for the last two months. Instead of the tall buildings, he had become used to seeing endless fields with tall coconut and palm trees. The single-lane roads which were occasionally blocked by a herd of cows or sheep were a far cry from the multi-laned roads brimming with vehicles.

"When are you planning on returning, son?" Vikram's mother asked.

Vikram turned to look at her. "I'll fly back in a week."

She let out a sigh. "I wish Vishal could've joined you, too."

Vikram knew that his mother was worried. Each time he or Vishal had spoken to her, she asked them to be careful and not to hurt the sentiments of Suryaprakash because of their charade.

But Vikram knew it was unavoidable. He only hoped that the older man would eventually understand why they had to do what they did.

Soon the car pulled into the large gates and drove through the driveway that led to the Saaho house. As soon as he got out of the car, Vikram went inside the house and took the stairs before heading straight to his grandfather's suite.

He knocked on the door twice, and then realizing that his grandfather was still not able to talk, he pushed the door open.

His grandfather was lying down on his bed while holding a book.

"Grandfather?"

As soon as Vishwanath Saaho looked at his older grandson, a small happy smile covered his face. "Vikram," he whispered.

Vikram took the chair that was right next to the bed. "How are you, Grandfather?" he asked.

"I'm... fine," he spoke in a faint whisper. "How is... Surya?"

"He is doing very well. You must already know that he leads a very active lifestyle. If you get better soon, you can visit him in your village."

Vishwanath Saaho smiled faintly and nodded.

Vikram's eyes briefly fell on the book his grandfather was reading. He realized it wasn't actually a book but a photo album.

"Surya and Bhanu..."

At his grandfather's words, he picked up the album and flipped through it. Most of them were childhood pictures of Vishwanath Saaho and Suryaprakash Gulati. There were a few with them during their teen and early twenties. When Vikram saw a picture of a woman laughing next to his grandfather, he knew she must have been Bhanumati Gulati. Sangeeta and her sister looked a lot like their grandmother.

"I... did... wrong." Vishwanath Saaho struggled to form the words. "I hope... Suri... forgives me."

"He will, Grandfather. He's a very generous man. Vishal and I will soon convince him to meet you."

The older man nodded with a pensive look. Vikram could see that he was struggling to stay awake.

"Take rest, Grandfather. I'll come by later."

Vishwanath Saaho didn't reply. He just held the photo album book and closed his eyes.

Covering his grandfather with a bedspread lying near the foot of the bed, Vikram stepped out of the suite.

For the next few hours, after Vikram freshened up, he caught up with work emails.

He was discussing a few agendas for the meetings with his father when there was a knock on the door.

Vinita Saaho stepped into the large office suite with a smile. "Still working?"

"Wrapping up now, darling," Rajesh Saaho replied.

"Hurry up. Vikram must be starving. He hasn't eaten anything since he arrived," she said.

Vikram followed his mother down the stairs while she led him to the dining room. Vikram did feel quite hungry. Especially when his mother went through the extra effort to have all of his favorite dishes prepared.

"So how do you like the life in a village so far?" she asked while serving him food.

"It's different," he replied.

She smiled. "I'm sure it is. I know you can adapt anywhere as long as you have phone access and you can work. But I'm surprised that Vishal seems to be in high spirits, working and living a life in a village."

"He knows it's temporary."

Vikram's mother laughed. "I really want to be a fly on the wall and see how you both had adapted to the village life."

Vikram smiled. "I do have pictures. I've asked Pooja to have someone arrange for printing the pictures that Vishal and I have taken recently in the village. Did those arrive?"

Vinita was surprised. "Yes, a small package was dropped off an hour ago. I thought it was something to do with your office work."

"No. I realized a while ago that Grandfather might enjoy seeing them."

"Oh, Papa definitely will. And also..." She looked hesitant and then there was a flash of determination in her eyes. "Speaking of pictures," she said. "I have a couple of pictures of some really wonderful girls. One is the daughter of an industrialist based in London. The other a software heiress based in the United States. I would like you to take a look."

"Mum. I'm not going to look at any of them."

At his matter-of-fact tone, Vikram's mother's expression fell immediately and she looked hurt.

"I don't want to, Mum," he said with a small smile, "because I already know whom I'm going to marry."

Vinita Saaho looked stunned. And then, a slow radiant smile burst on her face. "Who!"

"Sangeeta Gulati," he replied. "I haven't asked her yet. But she is the one I'm going to marry."

"Oh my God! This is great news, son. And, of course, she is going to say yes!"

Vikram smiled seeing his mother's excitement and happiness. "Let's hope so, Mum."

"Do you have her pictures? I have got to see my daughter-in-law right now!"

"The phone that I used in India is up in my room. I do have a few pictures of her in there. The pictures that I had printed to show grandfather, also has a few." Before he could finish, his mother got up from the chair and hurriedly went up the stairs.

Vikram let out a short laugh.

"Congratulations, son," Rajesh Saaho said with a pleased smile.

"Thanks, Dad. But I think it's a bit early. You know there might be complications when Suryaprakash finds out who Vishal and I are."

Rajesh nodded. "Yes. There's a good chance he might not take it well."

Vikram had spent enough time with Suryaprakash to know that the older man could be overly generous at times, but sometimes, he did hold on to his beliefs even if they weren't necessarily right.

A faint, excited shriek was heard from above. Most likely from his room.

"We better go up," Rajesh Saaho told his son in a dry tone. "Before your mother starts calling and booking your wedding venue,"

Vikram laughed.

As soon as he stepped into his bedroom suite, he saw that his mother had spread the pictures he and Vishal had taken in Srirampur across his bed.

"She's so pretty, son. And she's a doctor!"

"Suryaprakash has two granddaughters," Vikram stated in amusement. "How do you know which one is Sangeeta?"

"With this picture!" she said victoriously. "Anyone who sees this picture would know how you feel about Sangeeta." She held up the print of a picture which Vishal must have taken. It was during the Banni cultural festivities. Vikram was intently staring at Sangeeta.

Vikram laughed. "I think I need to see these pictures first before deciding which ones to show Grandfather."

"Why? Papa will be very happy to know you fell in love and want to marry his friend's granddaughter."

"Right now, Grandfather is our priority, Mum. I want to first focus on fulfilling his promise before anything."

His mother nodded in understanding. "So when can I talk or meet Doctor Gulati?" she pressed.

"She's not Doctor Gulati," Vikram softly told his mother. "She is Doctor Shetty. She was widowed last year."

His mother was stunned. And then, she shook her head. "Oh. My poor girl," she said looking at the picture in her hands. "Now I can't wait to give her a big, tight hug, too."

Vikram smiled. The next few hours were spent with his mother continuing to grill him about Sangeeta. She wanted to know what Sangeeta liked to eat. What she liked to wear. How she liked spending her free time. His mother finally took a break when a nurse informed them that his grandfather was awake.

Vikram immediately went to his grandfather. He took the copies of the pictures with him. During the rest of his visit, he showed his grandfather the pictures and spoke about the life in Srirampur. He also spoke about Suryaprakash.

"I miss... Srirampur," Vishwanath Saaho said. "Take me... home... Vikram."

CHAPTER THIRTY

The car stopped in front of Bhanu's college.

"I'm so late!" she said, turning to take her bag from the backseat. "See you." She was just about to get out of the car when she felt Vishal's hand on her arm.

She looked at him in surprise because he never touched her where they could be discovered.

"This," he said, pulling out a long, hay twig from her hair.

Bhanu fought a blush getting reminded of the earlier stop in the fields. "Thank you," she murmured before getting out of the car.

She stared at him for a few moments. With his dimpled smile and messy hair which was because she had pulled at it a few minutes ago, he looked way too tempting. She wanted to get back into the car.

He shook his head with a laugh. "Stop watching me like that and go! Otherwise I'm going to drag you back in and drive away from here."

Blushing once again, she turned away hurriedly and began to walk towards the classes.

Her friends along with the rest of the students were waiting outside.

"I thought I was late," she said. "Isn't it time already?"

"Yeah. But they are still checking the classrooms for cheat chits and other things before they begin the exam."

"Oh."

Bhanu's friend, Kavita, let out a deep sigh "I'm so glad we are going to be done with our final exams soon."

"But I'm sad that we'll all have to return home," another friend added. "I'm going to miss you all."

There were murmurs of agreement. "But we can all meet often. We all stay in the same city. Except for you, Bhanu."

"I'm going to miss you girls, too," Bhanu replied. "But most likely I'm going to be taking up a job in the city. So I can meet you all anytime, too."

There were excited shrieks.

"Where are you going to work?" Kavita demanded.

"I don't know that. I have just begun applying."

"When you come, make sure to bring Vishal along," said Kavita with a grin.

"What?" Bhanu's heart gave a leap. Did her friends suspect anything?

"Oh God, yes, please! Bring him along!" another friend said in an awe-filled tone.

Bhanu laughed at her friends' antics. "First, let's be done with exams and then we can discuss who I can and cannot bring along."

A bell rang loudly, indicating the exam would begin. Even as Bhanu walked inside to her classroom, she was looking forward for the day to be done, so she could go back to Vishal.

Since their first time in his room, four weeks of passion-filled days had gone by.

The days were filled with stolen kisses and hurried couplings, not just in his room, but also in the open fields and in every possible hidden place. And the thrill of danger of getting caught and their forbidden affair added to the passion.

So far, Bhanu hadn't allowed any other thoughts apart from Vishal's kisses and touch to fill her mind. She didn't want to think about the future. She didn't want to think about her job which would lead her closer to her goal. And she definitely did not want to think about the fact that she would have to end the affair with Vishal at some point.

But on some level, she knew she had to put at least some distance between them. Because each time she saw Vishal, her heart skipped a beat and not just her body, even her mind was beginning to crave him.

Vishal wasn't just devilishly handsome, he was also quite intelligent. Whenever she spoke to him about technology or some news regarding current affairs, he listened for the most part, but he did have quite good insights.

And what made it even scarier for her was that whenever she lay on her bed alone in her room, she always thought of Vishal. She had one persistent thought where she imagined how it would be to have Vishal in her life permanently.

Even now she wondered. Would it be so bad?

CHAPTER THIRTY-ONE

Vishal was in his room, speaking to his mother who seemed to be in high spirits because of Vikram's visit.

"Vikram is right, Mum. Now isn't the time to bring Grandfather to India. Give us a few more days, and we'll tell Suryaprakash who we are and then request him to meet his childhood friend."

"I miss you, son. When are you coming to visit us?" his mother asked.

"I miss you, too, Mum. And I'll try to come soon, too."

His mother continued to be excited. And then, she told him something that made him freeze on the spot. "Bro said what? Marry who?" he asked.

"Sangeeta! Suryaprakash's granddaughter."

Vishal was stunned. Vikram had told their parents that he wanted to marry Sangeeta?

Vishal knew that Vikram liked the older Gulati sister, but he had no idea that his brother was that serious. He wondered whether Sangeeta liked his brother, too. And how would Suryaprakash react to the news.

Vishal was about to ask his mother to pass the phone to his brother when he heard a sound coming from outside of his room. "All right, Mum. Someone's here. I'll have to call you back."

Ending the call, he stepped out of the room and entered the barn with a frown.

It was Bhanu.

Vishal was surprised. As soon as Bhanu saw him, she came running towards him.

Her body crashed into his, and he wrapped his arms around her before lifting her off the ground. She wrapped her legs around his hips while their mouths melded together.

They kissed as though they were starving. As though they hadn't had wild sex that morning out in the fields and also during that evening in the car while they were heading back home.

Vishal had stopped the car to the side of the highway and pulled Bhanu to him. She was more than willingly. And soon their moans and gasps had filled the car. But since Bhanu's exams were going on, they had to forcibly stop with one round. Or rather, he put a stop to it even though she didn't want to.

He recalled how Bhanu had blushed and was embarrassed because they had steamed up the car windows. Vishal had to get down the car and wipe away the moisture before they continued to drive back home.

With a great effort, he forcibly pulled his mouth away and pressed his forehead to hers. "Didn't we decide that you wouldn't come here tonight?" he stated in a stern tone. "Because you have to prepare for your finals tomorrow."

"*You* were the one to decide that, not me," she said with a small pout. "I have prepared enough for my exam and I know I'm going to top once again."

He laughed. "Arrogant, much?" he asked in a teasing tone. But it was followed by a groan when the wily seductress began to kiss along his jaw.

"Not half as arrogant as you," she stated. And then, she pulled him closer. "Take me inside," she commanded.

Grabbing on to her more tightly, he did as she ordered.

A month had passed since they began their torrid, passionate affair, but he was still addicted to the woman. Not just to her body, but also to her mind and company. She was fiery, stormy and smart. He loved holding on to all that passion and intelligence most of which was directed at him.

At first, he had thought that his attraction and fascination towards her would end as soon as he slept with her. He took her as many times as possible, hoping he would be sated. But it didn't work that way. If anything, his hunger for her grew even more.

He constantly wanted to be with her and talk to her. He listened to her when she told him of her interests in computers. She even shared with him the information on how she had received offers from top universities to pursue her dreams.

He had listened, but he didn't advice her because according to the charade, a driver wasn't supposed to know the intricate details of the various top universities and possible career options if she were to pursue her dream. He was biding his time to reveal the truth, so he could be her equal and have such talks.

He dropped her on the narrow bed and attacked her clothes. And as soon as he had her naked and willing, he pulled her under him.

Their joining was passionate like always. But lately, he was beginning to have strange urges. Urges such as not just wanting to give and take pleasure but also to cherish her.

As he drove hard and fast into her, he kissed her tenderly on her lips. She held his head and kissed him back the same way. Something strange and deep passed between the two as they maintained eye contact while he took her body. Instead of it being just sex, it felt as though they were making love. And instead of being scared shitless for even thinking that way, it actually felt right.

Much later, after both of them raced to their finish lines, he held her and rolled them, pulling her on top of him.

He let out a deep, content sigh as he held her and began to rub her back with his fingers.

Bhanu's face was at the crook of his neck and she was playing with the locket on his chest.

"Vishu..." she said.

He liked how she called him by that name sometimes. "Yes?"

"Do you want to remain as a driver all your life?" she asked.

He was surprised by her question and decided to answer it glibly. "I don't know, Princess. If being a driver would get me hot chicks like you, maybe I'll remain one."

"I'm serious, Vishu," she said. "Have you ever thought of starting your own business or doing something that will help you earn more? You have a decent brain with innovating thinking. I can even ask Grandpa to lend you some money to start a small business of your own."

He smiled. "Decent brain and innovative thinking, huh? That's quite a compliment coming from you, Princess."

She remained quiet.

He slowly sighed. He knew what the woman in his arms wanted to hear. "Yes. I do aspire beyond just being a driver."

He felt her smile against his neck. "Good," she murmured sleepily.

Vishal knew he should send Bhanu back to her room. They had been taking too many risks as it is. But Bhanu felt so good in his arms and it felt so right.

So he held her and continued to rub her back until her breathing deepened indicating she had fallen asleep in his arms.

CHAPTER THIRTY-TWO

"It's quite normal for you to feel these pains. They are not labor pains. There's still quite some time for those." Sangeeta smiled at the expectant mother. "Continue with those breathing exercises I taught you and keep drinking warm Tulasi tea."

The pregnant woman nodded before thanking Sangeeta and leaving.

Sangeeta sighed while rubbing the back of her neck. She wondered what the time was. As though on cue, her stomach rumbled a bit, indicating it was time to take a break for lunch.

"Kailash," she called out. "I'll be back in an hour. Let me know if a patient comes by."

"Sure," said Kailash who was sorting the medicines.

Sangeeta stepped out of the clinic and was about to head towards the kitchen when a deep, masculine voice called out, making her jump.

"Feeling hungry, Doctor?"

With her heart thumping crazily, Sangeeta turned. She drank in the sight of Vikram leaning against one of the outside walls of the clinic. He was holding a lunch carrier and had a small smile on his face.

"Famished!" she replied with a wide, happy smile.

"Then let's go," he said softly. He held her elbow in a gentle grip and guided her to their usual lunch spot. And then, he began to unpack the lunch.

"When did you get back?" she asked.

"Just now. I'm yet to meet your grandfather."

Her heart gave another crazy thump. "How is your grandfather? And how are your parents doing?"

"Everyone is doing fine." He paused in the act of serving her food to look at her. "I told my parents about you."

"Oh." She was excited and nervous about that fact. "What did you tell them? What did they have to say?"

His eyes gentled seeing her nervousness. "I told them that I met a beautiful and wonderful woman. They were very happy."

"Did you... did you tell them I was married before?" she asked hesitantly, knowing well that regardless of their social positions, most parents weren't too happy to have their sons be associated with a woman who had been married before.

"Yes," he replied softly. "That fact doesn't make a difference to me and neither did it make any difference to my parents."

She smiled, feeling extremely relieved. "Your parents sound wonderful."

He returned her smile. "Yes. They are, and they can't wait to meet you."

Sangeeta stared at Vikram, feeling in awe once again that this perfect, handsome man who captured her heart also wanted her in return.

While she stared at him, his smile vanished slowly and he returned her stare with a heated one. She felt her body tingling as her heartbeat sped up further.

They kept staring at each other, until a familiar voice called out, making Sangeeta jump once again.

"Vikram," Sangeeta heard her grandfather greet. "When did you return?"

"He came in just now, Grandpa," Sangeeta hurriedly replied. "His grandfather is doing fine and so are his parents. They seem very nice." She knew she was babbling, but she didn't seem to have any control of her mouth. "I just finished seeing a patient and was hungry. So he and I. We were... we were..." She was suddenly at a loss for words.

"Having lunch together?" her grandfather supplied.

"Yes! We were having lunch together. We always have lunch together when he's home around lunch time. Don't we, Vikram?"

Vikram looked amused. "Yes, sir. We do."

Suryaprakash Gulati laughed heartily. Sangeeta's cheeks heated.

Her grandfather looked at her with a smile and laid an affectionate hand on top of her head. "Enjoy your lunch," he said in an indulgent tone.

"Thank you, Grandpa," she said.

Her grandfather looked at Vikram. "I'm going to the neighboring village with Ravi for some official work," he said. "I'll talk to you later when I return."

"Yes, sir."

As soon as her grandfather left, she turned to Vikram who was watching her with an amused smile.

Her cheeks heated again.

Letting out a rich, masculine laughter, he said, "Let's eat."

Feeling happy and excited, she began eating. In between, she regaled him with what had happened during the week while he was away. Nothing major, it was just some silly and sweet stuff that had happened at the clinic and around the house. But as always, Vikram gave her all his attention and listened to her.

Soon, they were done with their meal.

Sangeeta wanted to stay and continue talking to Vikram, but she knew there would be patients waiting for her.

"Don't worry about me," said Vikram, reading her mind. "We can talk later."

She nodded. "See you later," she said, continuing to float in a cloud of happiness while she went back to the clinic.

***

Vishal was firing off an email to a lawyer when the door to his room opened.

"Someone seems impatient despite our last pit stop at the fields. I'll be right with you, Prin—" he broke off when he saw his brother standing inside his room instead of Bhanu.

Vishal grinned. "Welcome back, bro!" He got up and went towards Vikram to thump him on his back. "Mum told me. Congratulations are in order. I knew you took an instant liking to Sangeeta."

Vishal was really glad. Sangeeta was a perfect match for his brother and Vishal liked Sangeeta. She was sweet, friendly and always ready to help everyone in need. His grin widened. The other Gulati sister was also the kind to help everyone in need, but he could hardly classify her in the sweet and friendly category.

"How is Grandfather doing?" Vishal asked.

"He is fine." Vikram had a frown on his face. "But what are you doing?" he asked.

"Sending an email to the lawyer about the contract renewal for leasing—"

Vikram cut him off. "I meant what the hell are you doing with Bhanu?"

Vishal automatically clammed up. He wasn't willing to discuss Bhanu to anyone. Not even to his brother with whom he was quite close to.

"Are you sleeping with her?" Vikram demanded. "You know damn well she isn't like the women you are used to who know what they are getting into beforehand. Bhanu is an innocent."

Vishal felt irritated at the truth. "I know that, all right."

"Then why the hell are you continuing? What are your intentions?"

Vishal took a deep breath. "Marriage," he stated. "My end game is to make Bhanumati Gulati fall in love with me and marry me. I—" he broke off when he heard a loud gasp.

Frowning, he turned to the source of the sound. Bhanu was inside the barn. She must have just arrived like they had planned beforehand.

There was a complete shock on her face. "Your end game is to make me fall in love with you and then get married?"

Vishal frowned. "That's not how I meant it—"

She let out a sob and flew towards him. Instead of jumping into his arms like always, she slapped him hard. "Go to hell! I hate you!" Spitting out those words, she stormed off.

Vishal went after her. "Bhanu, wait! You misunderstood me."

But she was too quick. She ran out of the barn and disappeared into the house.

He couldn't shout her name out loud. So he quietly followed her until she went into her room and banged the door shut.

He waited outside helplessly. "Bhanu," he called. But there was no response. He called out her name a few more times and got no reply.

Unable to bang on the door or make a spectacle, he slowly turned away to return to his room.

Vikram was still standing inside the barn. "She thinks you deliberately tried to trap her."

"I know, Dammit!" Vishal pinched the bridge of his nose. "This is so fucked up. How do I convince her otherwise? Without telling her the whole damn truth?"

"You can't. At least not now when we are very close to having Suryaprakash listening to us."

"Dammit!"

***

Bhanu felt utterly shocked and betrayed. Yes. It was betrayal. There was no other word for what he did.

She tried hard to ignore the ache in her chest and the hollow feeling in her stomach as though someone had kicked her hard.

How could he! While she was falling for him, he was simply playing with her emotions so he could trap her into marriage.

Bhanu realized she was crying when she tasted the salty tear drops. Furiously, she wiped her face.

I am not going to cry! Not for that cheat!

And it served her right. She fell in love with him even though it didn't fit in with her plans. She was even dreaming of building a life together with him. But now that she had discovered his betrayal, it set her straight.

She pulled out her phone and furiously typed. She was going to accept the job offer.

CHAPTER THIRTY-THREE

Vishal continued to cool his heels outside the main house. Bhanu didn't pick up his calls or even come out of her room for the entire day. She had told Lakshmi and her sister that she wasn't well and was resting. All her meals were taken inside her room.

Vishal waited impatiently. Just when he thought he was going to march into the house to break down her damn door, consequences be damned, Bhanu finally came out of her room.

She threw him a cool look before walking towards the barn.

He followed her inside.

As soon as they were shut off from the rest of the household, he immediately went close to her. "Bhanu... Princess... I—" Before he could finish, she cut him off.

"I had time to think about this," she said. "I now know that you are trying to trap me into marriage. And I also know that if I don't agree, you might even blackmail me."

Vishal frowned. "What?"

"You blackmailed me before and you are more than capable of doing it again."

He couldn't believe that she thought that way about him. "If you recall, *you* came to *me*, Princess. *You* demanded that I teach you to kiss. *You* demanded that I bloody show you how to make love. *You* were the one sneaking into my bed."

He could see her get embarrassed. But she pulled on a stubborn look before ignoring his statements and continuing with her ridiculous accusations. "I know that you wanted to use me as a stepping stone or whatever opportunist men like you do with women like me."

"But you are not rich," he pointed.

"I'm richer than you!" she snapped. "And I'm sure you found out quite a lot regarding my assets through my grandfather. He must have told you that I own some land in the village and have a small trust fund on my name left to me by my parents. Well, it's too bad your plan won't work. I already made my own plans that don't include you."

His frown increased. "What plans?"

She sucked in a deep breath. "Ashok Vadani," she said.

"Who the hell is that?"

"Owner of Vadani Industries," she replied. She even gave the bloody statistics of the company's revenue.

"Ashok Vadani is forty five years old and a widower," she continued. "I'm going to be his mistress. There's an open position for a personal assistant in his company. I've applied for it and I'm hoping to get the job soon."

Vishal saw red. He wanted to smash something into pieces. Either that or drag the woman in front of him to his bed and spank some sense into her head.

"Why are you still pursuing that stupid idea of being a rich man's mistress?" he snapped. He wanted to yell that his inheritance was easily over several hundred times than that bloody man's whom she was vying for.

She raised her chin. "It's not a stupid idea," she said. "And I never for a moment considered not pursuing it."

"Like hell, I'll allow that," he growled. "You are mine!"

Her eyes narrowed. "I'm not yours. Or any man's," she said.

His arm caught the front of her dress and pulled her to him. Ignoring her shocked gasp, his hand clasped her jaw before his mouth settled on hers possessively. He kissed her.

When she was unable to breathe and only when he was ready to let her go, he raised his mouth from hers.

"Princess," he said in a dark tone. "The moment you let me inside your body, you became mine. Now all you have to do is to acknowledge that you let me into your heart, too."

She looked dazed as she always did when he kissed her. But soon, she shook her head, looking visibly shaken and uncertain. "No. I don't love you. And I won't allow you to snatch my dreams away from me," she said.

He gritted his teeth, angry that she fought her feelings. "And your dreams are to be a rich man's mistress?"

She lowered her eyes, unable to meet his furious ones.

"Yes," she said, continuing to argue. "It's not just about me. I want Geeta and Grandpa happy, too. What can you offer me if I marry you? I'll probably have to move out of the main house and live here in the barn room with you. And Geeta and I will still continue to be poor relatives who would have to depend on scraps thrown to us by my uncle and his wife."

"Stop being so bloody materialistic and think of your happiness first," he snapped. "I can take care of myself and support you too without the help of your bloody inheritance. Why can't you pursue your dream of doing your Masters Degree and then earn a good job which pays well? You can take your sister and grandfather to whatever place with that money."

"I can't leave them here by themselves," she said in a small voice. "My sister passed out from the best medical school and became a doctor. People who are not half as good or brilliant as her earn way more money than her. She sacrificed a lot to stay with my grandfather and me. By the time I complete my Master's Degree, find a job and settle down, it'll be too late."

"You'll only be twenty-four or at most twenty-five for God's sake. Why is that too late?"

"You don't understand," she said, continuing to argue. Then she shook her head before taking a deep breath. "Forget it. It's not my goals we are discussing. All I want you to know is that you won't succeed in your goals to trap me. Even if you blackmail me or tell everyone about our affair, I'll never marry you."

They seemed to be arguing in damn circles. Vishal knew she was simply lashing out at him because she was hurt and scared.

He then suddenly knew what to do. Nothing like old-fashioned jealousy to set everything straight.

Yes, he was going to be manipulative, but everything was fair in love and war. And right now, it was both.

Bhanu Gulati was his. He would fight for her. He would be damned if he was going to let anyone come in between them—including the woman he loved.

He took in a deep breath before slowly putting on a thoughtful look on his face. "You are right. I did try to trap you." Her face fell and she looked devastated.

"But since you are on to me now," he continued. "I need to work faster." He stared at her for a few moments. "How does your friend Kavita feel about me? Do you think she would be receptive to—" Before he could finish, Bhanu came at him with a murderous look.

He caught her in his arms, and turned them around, until he had her back pressed against a wall. Her eyes were at the level of his, and so her feet didn't touch the ground. He kept her pinned using his body.

"You are lucky that I prefer aggressive and stubborn brats," he said with a grin, bringing his face closer to kiss the hell out of her.

But she turned her face away. "Get off me! I hate you!" she snarled.

Those words hurt him even though he knew she didn't really mean them.

His lips grazed her soft cheek. "But I love you, Princess," he said. "And I don't care whether we get married or not. All I want is you."

She fell quiet and slowly the tension left her body.

She turned her face to look at him. He stared back at her with an open look that bared his heart and soul.

She still looked scared and worried. "This wasn't supposed to happen," she whispered.

He gently cupped her cheek. "I know, Princess. But it did. And we'll somehow make this work."

He bent down and kissed her. This time it was a sweet kiss. Slowly and tentatively she kissed him back.

But soon, and as expected, their kiss turned hot and heavy. He felt her hands creep under his shirt, about to pull it up to take it off. But he pulled his lips away from hers and held her face. "Say it," he ordered.

She didn't hesitate. "I love you," she said softly.

He felt happy along with the feelings of deep possessiveness towards her. She was finally his. The woman he was going to grow old with.

With a wicked smile, he bent down slightly before throwing her on his shoulder.

She laughed and clutched his clothes as he carried her into his room. But soon the laughter turned into breathless gasps.

CHAPTER THIRTY-FOUR

Almost a week later, the head of the Gulati household summoned for Vikram and Vishal.

"Yes, sir?" Vikram asked politely. He tried hard not to look towards where Sangeeta was standing with her sister. But it was hard.

He looked at her and she began to blush. He knew he should tone down the intensity of his stare, considering her sister was standing right next to her. Luckily, her sister was busy staring at Vishal.

Vikram heard someone clear their throat. It took him a moment to realize it was Suryaprakash.

Vikram looked at the older man. "I'm sorry, sir. I was thinking of something. You were saying?"

Suryaprakash smiled. "I haven't said anything, yet. I was waiting for your attention. Now that I have it, I wanted to let you know that I would like to meet your parents."

Vikram was taken aback. "My parents, sir?" Vikram had no idea why Suryaprakash wanted to meet them. Did he want to convince his parents to move to Srirampur?

"Yes. Your parents," Suryaprakash stated. "According to tradition, the groom's side of the family is supposed to visit the bride's side to have the initial marriage talks."

There was a stunned silence.

Vikram, Vishal and both the Gulati sisters were staring at Suryaprakash with shock. And in turn, the older man seemed amused.

Suryaprakash looked towards his granddaughters. "That is if you agree."

"Yes!"

"Yes!"

Both Sangeeta and Bhanu replied at the same time. Their eyes widened and each of them looked at one another in shock.

Suryaprakash burst out laughing. "Looks like despite being so close to each other, both of you had no idea about the other being in love. I guess love does make you blind to everything around you. But luckily for you, I'm not blind. I could practically see the four of you falling in love."

Suryaprakash turned to Vikram and Vishal. "I'm not going to lie. I was very skeptical at first for obvious reasons. But after having seen you and spoken to you both, I am quite impressed. I like your humbleness and the fact that you are so well-suited in temperaments to my granddaughters."

Suryaprakash smiled. "Just so you know, I'm not a selfish man. If you two choose to quit your jobs or even want to move back to the city for better opportunities, I would still think you are the right choices for my granddaughters."

Suryaprakash got up from the chair. "All right. I'll leave you four to discuss and celebrate. Meantime, I'll call my son and his wife and ask them to visit us when your parents are here."

As soon as Suryaprakash left, Sangeeta looked at Bhanu with a wide smile and hugged her. "You sneak!" she accused.

Bhanu laughed and hugged her back, happy and excited that her sister was going to get married again and this time with a man she loves. That fact that Vikram and Vishal were brothers made it all the more exciting.

A little later, they were seated in the courtyard where Vikram and Sangeeta usually ate lunch together. Vishal and Bhanu joined them too that day.

"Tell me about your mother," Bhanu demanded.

"Well... she's quite sweet and giving," Vishal replied. "But sometimes, she could be sneakily stubborn and badger you until you'd cave and give in to her wishes. Ask Vikram, she had been trying to get him married for the last few years."

Sangeeta had an amused smile. "Oh. Surely not years?"

"Yup. Bro is quite picky. But I'm glad he was."

Sangeeta smiled at Vishal. "Thank you."

"Do you think she'll like me?" Bhanu asked Vishal in an eager tone.

Vishal grinned. "You are more of an acquired taste, Princess."

Bhanu hit him on his arm playfully.

Sangeeta smiled. "What about your father?" she asked.

"He's cool. As long as our mother is happy, he doesn't bother much about anything else. He's crazy about her."

"Aww... that's so nice," Bhanu said.

"Are you close to anyone else in your family?" Sangeeta asked.

"Our grandfather," Vikram replied softly. "He's the head of our family. We all respect him, and we also respect his rules and wishes."

Bhanu had a frown. "He sounds intimidating."

"Yes," Vishal replied. "Grandfather can be quite intimidating to strangers. But I know he'll automatically love you and Sangeeta because of who you are."

"Because of who we are?" Sangeeta asked in a puzzled tone.

"He meant because you are both our choices," Vikram replied.

"Oh." Sangeeta smiled. "When can they all come?"

"As soon as Grandfather is well enough."

***

Much later in the evening, the Saaho brothers were in a dilemma.

When they began their charade, they had never imagined this to be the scenario. The worst thing they had predicted before starting their charade was not to be able to fulfill the promise. But now, the worst thing was the possibility of losing Sangeeta and Bhanu.

"Or maybe we can ask Mum and Dad to come disguised as well," Vishal said. "And once we are married, we can reveal the truth. I know it's wrong, but I don't want to take chances and lose Bhanu because of an old man's stubbornness."

What Vishal suggested was quite tempting.

"No," said Vikram. "We might have fallen in love while pretending, but we can't marry pretending to be someone else."

Vishal fell silent as he thought it through. "Fine," he said with a sigh. "We are going to have to put to use all of our convincing and negotiating skills. Not just with Suryaprakash, but with Bhanu and Sangeeta, too."

Vikram nodded.

He called his father and told him about the conversation Suryaprakash had with him and Vishal that morning.

"I know it's risky, Dad. But this is the only way we can get them to meet each other."

"All right, son. Papa is eager to visit Srirampur. But we'll take him with us until the city. Once Suryaprakash meets your Mum and me, and we can convince him, we can bring Papa to Srirampur."

"Yes. That's a good plan. I'll let Suryaprakash know that you'll be arriving in two days."

CHAPTER THIRTY-FIVE

The Gulati household was buzzing with activity. Even though it wasn't a wedding or even an engagement ceremony, the fact that Sangeeta and Bhanu's future in-laws would be arriving, caused a lot of excitement.

The doors were decorated with flowers and a feast was being prepared for well over a hundred people who were mostly from the village.

Amidst the excitement and good wishes, there was one big downer. It came in the form of Uma Gulati.

"This is indeed such good news," Uma Gulati said with a wide, fake smile.

But Uma Gulati's husband wasn't too happy. "I can't believe this, father," Dharam Gulati said with a thundering frown. "How can you think of getting your granddaughters married to an accountant and a driver! We'll be a laughing stock if anyone finds out."

"Now, now. Dharam," Uma Gulati seemingly admonished her husband. "Times have changed. There is no more class or social system when it comes to falling in love. Papa is doing the right thing."

Suryaprakash smiled at his daughter-in-law. "You are absolutely right, Uma. Geeta and Bhanu love those two boys. That's all matters."

Bhanu was taking in the exchange quietly. She wanted to gag at the pretence her aunt was putting up.

As though the older woman could sense the sneering looks directed at her, she looked at Bhanu. Uma Gulati's smile widened before she hurried towards Bhanu and Sangeeta.

"My dears," she said. "How pretty you both look in such... antique saris."

"Thank you," said Sangeeta with a bright, happy smile.

But Bhanu heard the condescending tone when the word 'antique' was used. "Sangeeta is wearing our mother's sari and I'm wearing grandmother's. They not only hold sentimental value to us, but they are also aesthetically beautiful. Unlike some people, we chose not to exchange the saris we inherited to buy new ones."

Uma Gulati's eyes hardened even as she continued to smile. "You know, my dear, Bhanu," she said. "When your grandfather called to tell us that you would be getting married soon, and that the groom worked as your driver, I was very happy. Very, very happy. You deserve everything you earned."

The older woman put on a faux puzzled look. "But I wonder where you are going to live after the wedding. Here, in my house? Dharam and I were thinking of starting the renovations sooner, so I don't know if we can accommodate a whole lot of people living in the house while the construction is going on."

Sangeeta was quiet. Bhanu felt angry. She hated that she was allowing her aunt to spoil her and Sangeeta's happy day. But slowly, a doubt crept into Bhanu's mind. She was madly in love with Vishal, but she didn't think she would be able to stomach it if her aunt were to humiliate or embarrass Vishal or his brother. And Bhanu was quite sure that her aunt wouldn't spare even the remotest of chances to do exactly that in the near future.

"Where are the future grooms, anyway?" Uma Gulati asked. "I didn't really notice their presence the last time I was here. In my eyes, they were just help. And everyone knows that the help are usually invisible." She let out a laugh that grated on Bhanu's nerves.

"Ah. There they are," Suryaprakash Gulati's voice boomed right then.

Vishal and Vikram stepped into the house, joining the rest of the people.

As soon as Bhanu saw Vishal, all of her doubts vanished. The moment he stepped in, he looked for her. And as soon as he found her, she could see a flash of heat and tenderness in his gaze while his eyes swept her from top to bottom.

Bhanu couldn't tear her eyes off of him, either. He looked majestic even though he was wearing simple traditional wear.

"Oh... Oh my," Uma Gulati exclaimed.

Bhanu frowned, bracing herself to listen to her aunt pass yet another sarcastic or derogatory remark. But Uma Gulati's eyes had widened as the older woman took in Vishal and Vikram's appearances.

"Well," her aunt said in a predictable tone. "I can see the appeal, I guess. Tall, muscular, low-class men instigate quite a forbidden attraction. My Varsha's groom will be more elegant and classy."

Before Bhanu could snap back at the woman, she was distracted by the loud buzz of conversations in the room.

"What's that?" Uma Gulati asked with a frown.

The rest of the guests also looked confused and wondered what the source of the noise was.

It was a whirring sound. And it was getting quite louder.

Most of the guests stepped out of the house to see what it was.

Bhanu remained inside along with Sangeeta. Vishal and Vikram also stayed back.

"What do you think is that?" Bhanu asked Vishal when he joined her.

"It's a chopper," Vishal replied.

Bhanu was confused. "As in a helicopter?"

"Yes."

"But why would it come here?" Sangeeta asked in confusion as well.

"Let's go outside." Vishal held Bhanu's hand and pulled her along with him until they stood outside the door.

A helicopter landed outside in the large open land across the house. When the door was opened, a well-dressed, middle-aged couple emerged.

"I wonder who they are," Suryaprakash Gulati remarked in general.

"That's our mother and father," Vikram replied.

Bhanu was shocked and confused. Why would Vishal's parents come in a helicopter?

But Suryaprakash Gulati wasn't confused. All of a sudden, he appeared angry. "Who are you?" he demanded.

"We are Vikram and Vishal Saaho. Vishwanath Saaho's grandsons."

At Vikram's reply, the older man became furious. "How dare you! Get out!" he shouted. "Get out of my house and never return!"

Bhanu began to panic. And so did Sangeeta. "What's wrong, Grandpa?" Sangeeta asked urgently.

"The men you and Bhanu fell in love with are cheats. They lied to us about who they are. They are not from a humble family. They are one of the richest people in the world. The great Vishwanath Saaho's grandsons. The man I hate the most!"

Bhanu was shocked. "Vishal!" she said. "What's happening? Tell Grandpa he's mistaken."

"Your grandfather is speaking the truth," Vishal replied. His voice held a note of regret. "My brother and I came here under false pretences to fulfill our grandfather's wish. He wanted us to convince your grandfather to meet him."

His words hit Bhanu like a punch. "All of this... was pretence..." she whispered.

"Not all of it, Bhanu," Vishal held her hand in a firm grip. "What we had between the two of us is real."

"Leave Bhanu's hand!" Suryaprakash ordered.

Vishal's hand didn't drop away despite the order. Bhanu tried to pull her hand free, but he didn't let go. "Bhanu," Vishal said urgently. "You have to trust me."

Bhanu shook her head, unable to digest the truth. *The man I fell in love with doesn't even exist.*

She felt hurt and betrayed. Her eyes immediately sought her sister's. Sangeeta looked equally shocked and devastated.

Violently tugging her hand free from Vishal's grip, Bhanu went to her sister.

"Please hear us out, sir," Vikram was trying to convince Suryaprakash. "We didn't mean any harm. It was the only way we could get you to meet our grandfather. He wants to—"

"I don't care!" Suryaprakash thundered. "You thought wrong! I will never meet him willingly and you can never heal the rift between us. Get out of my house!" He looked at Bhanu. "Bhanu. Take Sangeeta inside and remain there."

With a nod, Bhanu led Sangeeta. But before she stepped into the house, she turned briefly to look back at Vishal. He was watching her with a helpless imploring look.

Lies. All lies!

An involuntary sob escaped her, but she took a deep breath to control herself.

"We'll get through this, Geeta. I know we will." Even as Bhanu said that, she wondered whether she was saying those words to console her sister or herself.

***

Vishal tried to convince the older man. "Sir. Please listen—"

"I asked you and your brother to leave this house right now!"

Rajesh Saaho joined his sons and tried to convince the older man as well. "Mr. Suryaprakash. Please. Try to understand. My father is not well. He wants to—"

"No! And I don't care whether he is well or not! Leave and save your dignities. Or I'll have my people use undue force."

150

"But, my father—"

"Dad," Vikram interrupted his father. "Let's leave."

"But, Vikram, it's not just Dad. You and Vishal are in love with—"

"We'll discuss this later, Dad," Vishal added. "Let's leave. Mum is upset."

Vinita Saaho was waiting by the helicopter with a helpless, tormented look. It was obvious even from a distance that things didn't go as they had hoped.

Slowly, Rajesh Saaho did as his sons asked. They went back to the waiting helicopter.

"What happened?" Vinita asked anxiously.

"He didn't take it well," Rajesh informed his wife. "We were prepared for this scenario, too. So let's just do what we planned. Let's give Suryaprakash time to cool off."

Vinita nodded.

The ride back to the city was quiet.

CHAPTER THIRTY-SIX

Three weeks passed by since the Saaho family flew out of Srirampur. Life as they knew before continued. Vikram and Vishal immersed themselves in work while meetings, calls and starting their ventures in India took up a significant amount of time.

Vishal was attending a party along with his parents and brother. The party was thrown in honor of the Saaho family by most of the city bigwigs.

"I'm so glad you are deciding to move some of your operations to India, Mr. Saaho."

"This is my father's birthplace," Rajesh Saaho replied. "As my sons have mentioned before, we want to explore and expand in the current Indian marketplace."

"We are waiting to meet the legendary Vishwanath Saaho. His life is quite an inspiration to many. When will he be able to join us?"

"Soon, I hope. He is still recovering from his stroke."

"Excuse me," said Vishal. He stepped away from the group and headed inside.

Vishal stopped in front of the bar and asked for a drink. While he waited, he pulled out his phone and dialed Bhanu's number. It rang continuously, and as expected, the call was ignored.

How can she just cut everything off so easily? It was almost as though the last three months had never even happened.

Feeling worked up, he downed the peg of expensive scotch in a gulp before asking for another one. He kept calling Bhanu's phone and downing a few more shots.

"Hi, Vishal."

Vishal stared at the glass of scotch he held in his hands. He was reminded of the drink he had in Srirampur. It probably cost a fraction of the single malt whiskey he was currently gulping down in shots. But that cheap alcohol had given one hell of a kick compared to the useless and expensive whiskey.

"Vishal?" the woman's voice called him again.

Slowly, with slightly bleary eyes, he turned towards the source of the voice.

"Hi," the woman said. "Remember me? Shika. We met at the hotel lobby a couple of months ago when you had come for signing the contracts."

Vishal vaguely recalled seeing the woman. "Yes? How can I help you?" he asked. Luckily his voice was still steady.

"I heard your family will be moving here to India permanently. I wanted to say that's quite thrilling and not to mention, awesome news."

Although nothing was quite finalized, the rumors began because the entire Saaho family was visiting India.

Vishal gave a noncommittal shrug. He didn't want to agree or disagree and begin a flurry of more speculations.

"Can I join you?" the woman asked.

Vishal shook his head. "I'm sorry. I'm not a good company right now," he said. He wanted to be left alone to brood in peace.

There was husky laughter. "Oh. Don't worry, I know the perfect way to lift your spirits," she said. "Why don't you come home with me?"

Vishal didn't have the patience to come up with an excuse.

"Sorry. I'm not interested. I'm already in a committed relationship," he said.

The woman laughed. "I know you aren't," she said. "Remember, I did some research on your background before meeting you. You never had any girlfriends or were never in any committed relationship."

"I am now."

"Really? And where does your girlfriend live? London? Paris? Well, even if you have a girlfriend, she is not here right now, is she? What we do tonight will always remain a secret. No one has to know."

Vishal was annoyed. "The woman I'm committed to lives in India. And I have no intention, nor the interest to cheat on her."

The woman had a skeptical look. "Oh. Is she here at the party right now? I didn't see you arrive with a woman apart from your mother."

"She isn't here. She lives in a village."

The woman burst out laughing. "That's a good one. Vishal Saaho falling in love with a woman who lives in a village." She gave him a knowing look. "Your conquests outside the boardrooms are well known, Vishal. No one in their right mind would ever believe you."

A flash of doubt crept into Vishal's mind. Did Bhanu look up information about him on the internet? And if she did, things she would read about his personal life would make her loathe him.

He was doing it all wrong! Maybe he should not give her time. It would only make her fall out of love with him. He needed to hurry up and get her.

He got up from the bar stool. "Excuse me," he said. He didn't bother to turn when the woman called out to him. He just needed to speak with Bhanu right then.

He dialed Bhanu's number again. Surprisingly it was answered. "Bhanu," he said. "I—"

"Bhanu is sleeping. This is Lakshmi, Vishal."

"Wake up Bhanu, Lakshmi. I want to talk to her."

There was a pause. "I don't think she will agree to talk to you, Vishal. I answered the phone to let you know that Suryaprakash is trying to get Bhanu married to someone soon. The groom and his family have already come and seen her. They even told Surya that they liked Bhanu and would like to fix a wedding date soon."

Rage erupted in Vishal's mind. "Tell Bhanu I'm coming to get her!"

He ended the call and dialed Tanuj's number. Even though it was well past midnight, the other man answered. "Arrange for a ride, Tanuj. I need to go to Srirampur."

"Sure, Vishal."

While Vishal waited for the arrangements to be made, he scrolled through the pictures he had on his phone for what seemed to be the millionth time.

He and Bhanu belonged together. He was going to bring her home and keep her with him until the older man agreed to their marriage. And if he didn't, Bhanu and he would marry without permission.

Vishal was pacing on the lawn outside when his brother joined him.

"Where are you going?" Vikram asked.

"To Srirampur. To bring Bhanu back with me."

"Vishal. You know it's only going to make things worse. Let's bide our time and allow things to cool for a while. Grandfather will get better by then, too."

Vishal looked at his brother's face. His brother looked cool and reserved as usual. But they were bonded by blood, so Vishal could see past the surface. "Tell me the truth. How do you feel not being with Sangeeta these past three weeks?"

Vikram remained silent for a few seconds before answering quietly and matter-of-factly. "Like my fucking limb has been missing and my heart has been ripped out."

Vishal smiled. It was a bitter smile. "Love has managed to make even a man like you into a poet, brother." He shook his head to stop the world from spinning. "I love Bhanu. And I cannot sit passively waiting for some miracle to happen while she is being forced to marry someone else."

He began pacing again while waiting for the call informing of the arrangements.

"You can't go alone in this condition. I'll come with you," said Vikram.

CHAPTER THIRTY-SEVEN

They took a car to Srirampur as Vikram didn't want to draw unnecessary attention to the Gulati house. By the time they arrived, it was close to seven in the morning.

This time when the Saaho brothers stepped inside the Gulati household, they were dressed the way they usually were. They were wearing the same three-piece suits from the party the night before.

"I'm going to Bhanu," said Vishal.

Vikram nodded and went towards the clinic.

Sangeeta was standing outside. She was staring at something with a lost look.

The first sight of her hit him like a punch. He noticed that she had lost weight and had dark circles under her eyes.

"Sangeeta."

She turned towards him, and when she saw him, she didn't immediately react. She looked at him with slow, blinking eyes as though she was trying to decide whether he was really there or she was hallucinating.

Going closer, "How are you, Sangeeta?" he asked.

She looked at him for a few more moments until she burst out crying.

Immediately, he pulled her into his arms, but at his first touch, she stepped away. She wiped her tears away and looked at him with equal amounts of hurt and determination.

"Why are you here?" she asked.

"I'm here for you."

"Why? Are you still thinking of using me to convince my grandfather to meet yours?"

He fell quiet as watched her. "I agree that when I first came here to Srirampur, it was to convince your grandfather to meet mine."

Her face fell even more, but he continued with the truth. "You were never part of my plans, Sangeeta. But the more time I spent with you, I knew you are the one for me."

She took a deep breath. "Please stop, Vikram. I don't believe you and I can't trust you anymore," she said.

"Why not?" he asked gently.

She lowered her head before speaking. "I looked up information on you. There's quite a lot written about you and your family. Beautiful, sophisticated women have tried to get your attention and failed. You expect me to believe I was the one to finally catch your attention?"

"Yes."

At his firm and definite answer, she sucked in a breath. "Even if you genuinely feel we have something between us, it's not real. It's just infatuation. We have known each other for only three months."

He put a finger under her chin and raised her head until her tearful eyes met his. "I love you," he said in a firm tone. "This is not infatuation. Whether or not our grandfathers agree to put aside their old grudges and whether or not you believe that I love you, I know that I'm going to wait for you, however long it takes. I know we are meant to be together and grow old together."

Her lips trembled, and tears filled her eyes and spilled, but she didn't say anything. He gently brushed away her tears.

***

Vishal marched into the house.

"Bhanu!" he shouted. When he didn't see her anywhere in the living area, he went towards her bedroom. "Bhanu!"

He saw that her bedroom door was closed. He pushed it open and strode in.

Bhanu was seated on the edge of the bed. When she saw him, she didn't jump up to run into his arms as she had done in the past.

Vishal frowned seeing the spirited, passionate woman he fell in love in such a subdued manner. He was tempted to drag her into his arms and kiss her over and over again until she became animated once again.

He had to get her away from here. With that thought, he strode to her and held her wrist before pulling her off of the bed.

"Vishal... what are you doing..." Bhanu was in tears as she tried to pry his hands away.

"You are coming with me. I love you and I'm not letting you marry someone else!"

He dragged the struggling Bhanu with him. "Stop, Vishal," she pleaded. "Grandpa will—"

"I don't care," he said. "After we get married today, he'll have no choice but to accept the fact that he cannot come between us."

He heard her gasp. "What!"

He stopped and slowly pulled her close, cupping her face with his hands. "You still love me, don't you, Princess?" he asked.

Tears leaked out of her eyes as she nodded. "Yes," she whispered.

"I love you, too. Then what's stopping us from marrying today?" he asked before continuing to take her outside.

But before even he could take her to the waiting car, he saw another familiar car pulling right behind it. It was Suryaprakash.

The older man stepped out of his car. "Why are you here?" he demanded. "And where are you taking Bhanu?"

Vishal threw a challenging look at the older man. "Bhanu and I are getting married. We love each other. Just because you are a stubborn man, we are not going to sacrifice our love for your sake."

Suryaprakash wasn't angry. He appeared calm and collected. He looked at Bhanu. "Do you want to go with him? Or remain here with me?" he asked.

Bhanu looked at Vishal and then at her grandfather. Slowly, she let out a sob before looking at Vishal once again. This time with a torn look. "Let me go, Vishal," she whispered.

Vishal was shocked. And then, angry. "I won't let you sacrifice our love for the sake of an old man's pride!" He pulled Bhanu even closer. "You are coming with me and we are getting married today!"

"Vishal... please." She tried to pry her hand away from his grip. But Vishal didn't let her go.

Suryaprakash laughed coldly. "Well. Well. Aren't you just like your grandfather? Forcing and abducting unwilling women who don't want to be with you."

Vishal looked at the older man. "What are you talking about?"

Suryaprakash didn't reply. He looked at someone behind Vishal. "Take your brother and leave my village. I'm hoping that at least you have some modicum of decency and respect for your elders."

"Let's go, Vishal," Vikram said softly from behind.

Vishal was about to refuse his brother's request when he heard Bhanu's pleading voice. "Listen to your brother and please leave, Vishal. We are not meant to be," she said.

Feeling stunned, Vishal looked at Bhanu's tormented face. "How can you say that!" he shouted. "You just told me you love me!"

Bhanu didn't reply. She looked down, avoiding his eyes.

Feeling heartbroken, angry and dejected, Vishal slowly let go of Bhanu's wrist.

Bhanu raised her head to watch him with tear-filled eyes as though pleading with him to understand. "Vishu..." she whispered in a broken voice.

But Vishal wasn't moved anymore. He felt completely let down. Taking a deep breath, he followed behind Vikram into their waiting car.

And even while the car started and began to pull away, he kept his eyes firmly on the road and refused to look back.

***

Vikram remained silent during the ride, too. But just when they were about to leave the village limits, he received a phone call. It was from Lakshmi.

"*Vikram, please don't leave. I need to talk to you both,*" she said. She gave them instructions and asked them to wait near a small farmhouse that was in the village.

An hour later, Lakshmi joined them near the farmhouse.

"I'm sorry for what happened at the house," she said while leading them inside the farmhouse.

Vikram remained quiet. He knew Lakshmi hadn't come all the way to simply apologize. He waited for her to get to the point.

"I should have told this to you both before," she said. "But I didn't want to influence your opinion on either Suryaprakash or your grandfather. But now, I feel you have the right to know."

Vikram remained silent. And so did Vishal.

Lakshmi stared outside the small window as though she was lost in the past.

"As you both know, Surya and your grandfather were very good friends," she began. "Right from the age they could walk and talk, they were inseparable. Not a day passed when you wouldn't see them together. They went to the same school, lived in the same lane in the village, and had even promised each other that they would remain close friends even after they grew up and had families of their own.

"Even when they grew up, they maintained their close bond. They were very different in personalities and yet they complemented each other perfectly.

"Vishwa was the most handsome, the strongest and was also considered the most likely person to make it big in his life. He was very ambitious, your grandfather. He had big dreams, but one of his biggest dreams and wishes was to share his dreams with the girl he deeply loved since he was a child.

"While all the girls were in love with your grandfather, he was in love with Bhanu... He had been in love with her the moment he met her when they were barely ten.

"But Bhanu was oblivious to Vishwa's love. She only treated him as one of her best friends. Because the only person she loved since she was a little girl was Surya.

"Unlike your grandfather, Surya was more understated. He was calm and gentle with a big, charitable heart. Although Surya loved Bhanu too, he never let his feelings show because he knew his best friend was in love with her. Surya was ready to sacrifice his love for Vishwa.

"When Bhanu had confessed her love to Surya, Surya rejected it, telling her that he only considered her as his good friend and that she should not entertain any romantic notions about him."

Lakshmi let out a sigh. "Bhanu was heartbroken, but she waited for Surya to change his mind. And then, one day, things rapidly took a turn. Bhanu's parents tried to arrange her marriage with someone. Bhanu panicked, and she sent a letter to Surya through me on the night before the prospective groom's family was supposed to come and see her. In the letter, Bhanu had threatened to kill herself if Surya didn't come for her that night and marry her the next day."

Lakshmi looked at Vishal. "Bhanu was kindhearted and very sensible when it came to most things. But when it came to Surya, she was very stubborn and impulsive. Your Bhanu has that wild, impulsive streak in her like her grandmother. And like the previous Bhanu, your Bhanu loves her grandfather beyond reason, too. To the point that she can sacrifice anything and everything, just to please him and not to disappoint him. "

Vishal didn't respond.

"Where was my grandfather at that time?" Vikram asked. "When Bhanu's marriage was being arranged with someone else?"

"Vishwa had gone to the city to meet some people to set up a business. At that time, letters were the only means of communication. Bhanu's parents looking for a match, and Surya marrying Bhanu, all of it happened within a span of barely three days.

"When Vishwa returned to Srirampur and found out about Bhanu and Surya's marriage, he was furious. He more or less beat his best friend to a pulp for marrying the woman he loved. Surya didn't defend himself. He tried to explain the circumstances, but Vishwa wouldn't listen. Finally Bhanu's interference stopped Vishwa from almost killing his best friend.

"It was a bad time for Bhanu. She was not only ridden with guilt, but she was also heartbroken. Surya married her but wouldn't touch her or go close to her. He was too angry with her for making him choose between friendship and love.

"A few months later, Vishwa came drunk to Bhanu and Surya's house. He looked devastated. And in his drunken state, he tried to abduct Bhanu to take her with him to the city. Bhanu was terrified and tried to talk sense into Vishwa, but he wouldn't listen. Surya wasn't home then, but luckily before Vishwa could reach the city, Surya caught up with him. That was the only time Suryaprakash Gulati raised his hand on someone and was violent.

"After Surya rescued his wife and brought her home, no one heard from Vishwa again. The only information we all had was that Vishwa had left the country and made it big within a few years.

"Through the years, although Surya and Bhanu loved each other deeply and were happy, there was always that void of not having Vishwa around to share a part of their lives.

"Life went on, and Bhanu and Surya were blessed with two children, and soon they were busy with their small family. Years later, after Bhanu's younger son was married, Bhanu was diagnosed with a terminal illness. At that time, even though everyone was devastated with the news, Bhanu was not. She was content with her life. The only thing she wanted was to see Vishwa and make Vishwa and Surya be good friends again.

"Bhanu somehow tracked Vishwa's address and reached out to him. She wrote several letters requesting him to come and visit Surya and her. But Vishwa ignored all of Bhanu's letters and even phone messages.

"Bhanu passed away a few years later, holding the hand of the man she loved and surrounded by the family they had built. Surya was heartbroken. And later, when he found out that Bhanu had tried reaching out to Vishwa, but Vishwa ignored her multiple pleas, he was beyond furious."

Lakshmi looked at Vikram. "Two years ago, your grandfather reached out to Surya. He wanted to patch up. Later, Vishwa even proposed a marriage alliance between you and Sangeeta. But Surya was still angry, and in that anger, he had gotten Sangeeta married to someone else right away."

Vikram was taken aback. He had no idea that his grandfather proposed such an alliance.

"Please," the older woman said. "Have some more patience. I know Surya will come around soon."

Vikram nodded.

CHAPTER THIRTY-EIGHT

"Bhanu, the people from the prospective groom's side are getting impatient. So are your uncle and aunt. I want you to call Rahul and accept his proposal. He's going back to the United States in two weeks. I want you to get married by then."

Bhanu remained silent.

"Answer me, Bhanu. Will you get married according to my wishes?"

Before Bhanu could reply another voice shouted spoke in a firm tone. "No. She won't."

Bhanu was stunned. It was her sister. And she looked angry and determined. "Geeta..." Bhanu began.

"Don't stop me, Bhanu. I know you love Grandpa a lot and so do I. But I won't let you marry just anyone to pander to his pride, especially when you already love someone else."

"That's enough, Geeta," Suryaprakash said in a firm tone.

"It's not enough, Grandpa," said Sangeeta, looking more determined. "I married the man you chose without any questions because I had nothing to lose. I wasn't making any great big sacrifices. I trusted you and your judgment. But now, when it comes to Bhanu, I can't remain quiet knowing that this time your judgment is wrong."

"Geeta... please..." Bhanu tried to stop her sister from upsetting their grandfather.

"I'm not going to stop voicing my opinion today, Bhanu. Not when it comes to ruining your life just so Grandpa can prove his supremacy against his friend." Sangeeta looked at her grandfather. "We love you, Grandpa. We would do anything for you. But I love my sister, too. I will not let her be a sacrificial lamb to pander anyone's ego, not even if it is yours."

"Suryaprakash was quiet. "You don't know what happened in the past," he said finally.

"Maybe so. But nothing can possibly justify forcing Bhanu to marry someone against her wishes." She took a deep breath. "Lakshmi told me some of the things that had happened in the past. Yes, I agree Vishwanath Saaho was in the wrong when he ignored Grandma's last wishes. But I want you to know you are doing the same when it comes to him. What is the difference between you both? You are both allowing your egos and pride to come in the way of your friendship."

Suryaprakash's hand tightened on top of his walking stick when he heard his granddaughter say those words.

Bhanu knew he was upset and hurt. "Grandpa..."

Before she could go to him, he got up and walked away from the room.

Bhanu got up to go to her grandfather, but Sangeeta held her hand and stopped her.

"Geeta, Grandpa looked upset."

"I know. I regret causing him hurt with my words, but I don't regret saying them. He needed to listen to them and think them over."

Bhanu looked uncertain.

"Bhanu. I know you love Grandpa, but there is a limit to what you should do for that love. I'm telling you once again, don't ruin your future because of Grandpa or me."

Bhanu remained silent.

CHAPTER THIRTY-NINE

A week passed by and things remained at a standstill in the Gulati household. Although Suryaprakash and his granddaughters spoke to each other, there was a considerable strain between them.

Bhanu had just left with her college friends who had come home to take her away. Sangeeta was at the clinic and Suryaprakash was reading the newspaper after finishing breakfast.

"What's that sound?" Kamala asked while she cleared away the breakfast dishes on the table.

A familiar, faint whirring sound could be heard, and the sound slowly grew louder.

"It's a helicopter," Suryaprakash replied with a grim look.

He had thought Vikram and Vishal must have given up and returned to London for good.

Getting up from the chair, he slowly went outside and stood near the doorway.

A lot of people from the neighboring houses also began assembling outside to view the spectacle. Ignoring them, he kept his eyes on the helicopter. He knew it must be one of the Saaho family members come to convince him once again.

As soon as the helicopter landed, a young man got down first and put a small staircase near the door for the rest of the people to come out. Suryaprakash half expected to see Vikram or Vishal again, but he was shocked when he saw a man seated on a wheelchair. An old man with graying hair.

"Vishu..." The words automatically formed on his mouth.

He sucked in a breath as anger and happiness warred within him. He wanted to turn away and go inside his house and shut the doors firmly. But Sangeeta's words continued to resonate in his mind.

"What is the difference between you both? You are both allowing your egos and pride to come in the way of your friendship."

Taking another deep breath, he stayed still.

A middle-aged woman joined the older man and she pushed the wheelchair towards the house. Suryaprakash could see the wheelchair-ridden man taking in the familiar yet unfamiliar surroundings. It had been well over fifty years, and a lot had changed. Enough to overwhelm anyone who was connected and loved Srirampur as much as the wheelchair man did.

Suryaprakash recalled all the dreams and aspirations that Vishwanath Saaho had to develop their village. But along with it, Suryaprakash also recalled how after leaving Srirampur in a fit of anger and heartbreak, Vishwanath didn't bother to look back at all. Vishwanath had not only cut off relations with Bhanu and him, but also anything and everything that was related to Srirampur.

Guilt and anger began warring inside Suryaprakash.

The wheelchair stopped a few feet in front of the doorstep and the old man watched Suryaprakash quietly. The last time Suryaprakash had seen Vishwanath, they were both twenty-two years old. And now, seeing the heavily-lined face and slightly gaunt figure, it came as a shock to the system.

"How... are you... Suri?" Vishwanath Saaho asked in a halting voice with seemingly great effort.

Listening to that childhood name that only his best friend and his wife had used to refer to him, Suryaprakash felt overwhelmed. All emotions vanished except for the deep-rooted friendship and loyalty they had for one another during their childhood.

"I'm doing good, Vishu," he finally replied. He then gave a sweeping look over the wheelchair. "Looks like the reigning champion is temporarily disabled."

Vishwanath Saaho slowly smiled. "I can... still... win... over you... pal."

Suryaprakash laughed. Even at his old age, Vishwanath Saaho hadn't lost his overconfidence and cockiness.

"Come in," Suryaprakash invited his best friend into his home.

***

Sangeeta was at the clinic, cutting off the ends of a bandage on one of the village men when she heard the familiar noise. It was a helicopter.

Sangeeta knew what it meant and she wondered who had come from the Saaho family. She badly hoped it wasn't Vikram. And even if it was Vikram,

166

she hoped he would leave without meeting her. She didn't think her heart could take any more if she were to see him.

And if it was Vishal, then it was unfortunate that Bhanu wasn't home right then. Upon Sangeeta's bullying, Bhanu had just left with her college friends who had come home to take her away. Seeing Bhanu sad and listless had prompted Sangeeta to call some of Bhanu's close friends and request them to cheer their friend up.

Pushing away the speculation, Sangeeta focused on the task at hand. "Keep the bandage dry. Cover it with a plastic cover or sheet before taking your bath." She wrote down the medications on a notepad and tore the sheet. While she handed it over, she noticed another patient standing near the door and waiting for her.

Sangeeta smiled distractedly. "I'm almost done here. I'll be able to see you next," she told the woman.

As soon as the current patient left, the woman came inside. The woman was well-dressed and appeared to be middle-aged.

Sangeeta's heart began thumping when the woman smiled at her.

Although Vishal closely resembled his mother, Sangeeta could also see traces of resemblance between Vikram and his mother.

"Mrs. Saaho," Sangeeta greeted politely.

The older woman's smile widened displaying a set of dimples. "How did you know it was me?"

"Your sons resemble you."

"Ah, I see." The woman continued to smile warmly. "I'm Vinita. And you, my dear, look even prettier in person than in pictures."

Sangeeta felt awkward listening to that compliment. She didn't want to ask how and when the older woman had seen her pictures.

"Vikram showed them to me when he was visiting London two months ago."

Sangeeta remained quiet.

"Sangeeta, I know you and your sister must have been hurt when you found out the truth. But all I can say is that I know my sons. They would never deliberately set out to hurt any woman." Vinita Saaho held Sangeeta's hand. "Vikram really loves you, my child. He is deeply hurt and regrets hurting you."

Sangeeta felt a deep tug in her chest at the thought of Vikram feeling hurt.

Over the past month, she had indulged in quite a bit of self-pity and had only thought of how she had felt betrayed by Vikram. She hadn't imagined that the man she deeply loved was hurting similarly.

"Please don't think Vikram sent me here to convince you," Vikram's mother said. "In fact, my husband and sons have no idea that I brought Papa here."

Sangeeta was surprised.

Vinita Saaho smiled. "I know my husband and sons feel over-protective of Papa and want to shield him from being hurt. But I know Papa well, and he's quite resilient. And sometimes good old-fashioned nostalgia induced by face-to-face confrontation does a lot of wonders to set aside all differences."

CHAPTER FORTY

"Gentlemen, excuse us please." Rajesh Saaho stood aside waiting for his order to be followed.

Soon, the conference room was emptied except for him and both his sons.

"What happened, Dad? Is everything all right?" Vikram asked.

Rajesh Saaho shook his head as though in disbelief. "It's your mother. She took Papa to Srirampur."

Vikram and Vishal were taken aback.

"She said Papa is doing fine. In fact, she told me that Papa is inside Suryaprakash's house and they have been talking nonstop since morning." Rajesh laughed. "Here we are, looking for ways to convince Suryaprakash. And then, your mother just swoops in and goes for a direct attack. And damn if that woman's strategy didn't work." Rajesh Saaho sounded proud of his wife.

***

Vishwanath Saaho spent the entire day at the Gulati house catching up with his friend. They reminisced about their childhood adventures, especially the mischief that Vishwanath got into and dragged Suryaprakash into it.

When the sun began to set, the topic veered to the serious one.

"I'm... sorry," said Vishwanath. "I shouldn't... have... ignored... Bhanu's... letters." He looked at his friend straight in the eye. "I didn't... know... Bhanu was... dying."

Suryaprakash nodded.

"Do you... believe me?" Vishwanath asked.

"Yes. I do believe you... now. I was too blinded by grief of losing Bhanu and I directed that into anger towards you. I should have known you wouldn't ignore a dying woman's wishes. Especially of the one you cared deeply for in the past."

Vishwanath nodded.

"Let's set this right, Vishu," Suryaprakash suggested. "Let's set this right by giving into our grandchildren's wishes."

Vishwanath smiled. "Excellent... idea."

CHAPTER FORTY-ONE

Sangeeta's stomach rumbled.

It was close to three in the afternoon. Kamala had already come inside the clinic twice, trying to bully Sangeeta into taking a lunch break. Even though it was tempting, especially because she would be able to join her grandfather and his friend, Sangeeta did not agree. She wanted the old friends to continue with their bonding.

Sangeeta smiled. She had never seen her grandfather as happy as she had seen him in the last two days since his friend's visit. Both the men were behaving like small kids laughing and teasing each other.

Still smiling, she stepped out of the clinic, intending to go to the kitchen to pick her lunch carrier.

But a familiar voice made her legs freeze on the spot. "Feeling hungry, Doctor?"

With a sense of déjà vu, Sangeeta's heart thumped crazily as she slowly turned back.

Vikram was leaning against the outside wall of the clinic. He was holding a lunch carrier and had a small smile on his face. Unlike his last visit where he was dressed in an expensive three-piece suit, Vikram was now dressed in one of the shirts he had worn during his employment as an accountant.

"Famished!" Sangeeta replied with a wide, tearful smile on her face.

Vikram smiled. Carefully putting the lunch carrier down, he closed the distance between them and dragged her into his arms. And then, he kissed her.

It wasn't the sweet brushing of lips like he had done previously. This was a deep, passionate and intense kiss. It spoke of his longing. It showed how much he missed her. And most importantly, it also showed how much he wanted and loved her.

Sangeeta kissed him back. She wrapped her arms around his neck. With tears flowing down her eyes, she kissed him, showing him how much she missed and loved him.

After a while, he slowly raised his head, but didn't loosen his grip on her. "Marry me," he commanded.

Sangeeta laughed through her tears. "Aren't you supposed to ask me, not order me?"

"Habit," he said with a sheepish smile. Then wiping away the residual tears on her face, he gave her a lingering kiss. "I love you, Doctor Sangeeta. I promise to love you forever. Will you marry me?" he asked.

Sangeeta slowly smiled. "Yes!"

***

Bhanu's heart began to thud when she stepped out of her room and went towards the living room.

Lakshmi had just informed her that Vikram and Vishal had come to visit their grandfather and that Vishal wanted to speak with her.

Bhanu couldn't help but compare with Vishal's last visit when he hadn't bothered to ask for anyone's permission to see her and simply burst into her room to take her with him.

She inhaled a deep breath, but her stomach wouldn't stop its nervous flutter. As soon as she stepped into the living room, her eyes fell on Vishal. He was speaking with their grandfathers.

Bhanu drank in the sight of him. He looked different. Not just because of his expensive clothes.

The last time she had seen him, he was dressed in an expensive three-piece suit, but still he looked like her Vishal. But now, in his expensive casual wear, he somehow appeared distant and unattainable.

As though he could sense her presence, he looked up and saw her hovering near the entrance to the living room.

Her grandfather also noticed her. "Bhanu," he called out. "Vishal wants to speak with you."

Bhanu nodded.

Vishal stood up and walked out. She followed him as he led them to behind the house towards the barn, which was the only place that offered them some privacy.

Bhanu wanted to run into Vishal's arms and hug him tightly, but she restrained herself. A strange melancholy began to envelop her as Vishal continued to remain silent.

He stopped right outside the barn and turned to look at her. Bhanu stared back at the man she loved who was beginning to look too much of a stranger.

"My brother has proposed to your sister today, and we all know she loves him and will accept his proposal." He paused as though to gauge her reaction. Even though she was happy for her sister, she didn't show any outward reaction. She remained silent.

"Everyone is expecting me to do the same," he continued. "But that won't happen. Because unfortunately, I don't feel the same way as I did before."

Even though Bhanu had been expecting him to say these words, it still hit her like a blow in the stomach.

"I don't think we are meant to be or even well-suited to one another. Don't you agree?" he asked using the words she had used with him a few days before.

It hurt like hell, but she nodded her head in a jerky manner.

"I'm sorry if I hurt your feelings in the process," he said.

Bhanu remained silent unable to speak because she knew if she opened her mouth, she would bawl like a baby, and beg the man she loved to forgive her and to love her back.

"Since we will be closely related by family," he continued. "It would make it less awkward for everyone, if you tell your grandfather that you are the one who decided not to get married. And that you have your goals and certain plans for the future."

Shame and embarrassment hit her hard because he knew what her plans were before falling in love with him. She was sure he was recalling the time when she had told him that she wanted to become a rich man's mistress for materialistic reasons.

"I-I don't have those plans anymore," she said.

"Of course," he said politely as though he would give a damn either ways.

Had it been his anger or hatred, she could have at least begged him to listen to her explanation and ask for his forgiveness. But his indifference stopped her and hurt her more than anything. However, his indifference also gave her the much-needed strength, even though it was barely enough to stop her heart from feeling ripped apart.

She took a deep breath. "I'll tell my grandfather I want to pursue my Master's Degree. That was always my dream." She looked at him. "And don't worry. I will try not to make it awkward for anyone."

He nodded again with a polite look. "Well, all the best for your future," he said before turning and walking away from her life.

CHAPTER FORTY-TWO

Vikram and Sangeeta got married in Srirampur. Although they wanted a simple wedding, Suryaprakash Gulati and Vishwanath Saaho would hear none of it.

The entire village was decorated for the occasion. Everyone from the village was invited. And the Saaho's close family friends and associates were flown to Srirampur from all over the world.

Even though the wedding ceremony was simple, the celebrations were elaborate and lasted for more than ten days.

"My God! I think I will sleep through our entire honeymoon!" Sangeeta told her husband while staring out of the window of the private jet.

Vikram smiled. "I hope not *all* the time," he teased.

Sangeeta blushed.

"Take a nap. I'll wake you when we land," he said.

She nodded and with a sigh, she laid her head on his shoulder. Although she was nervous, she was tired enough to slip into a deep, content sleep.

She woke up when she heard Vikram's voice calling her.

"We are here," he said in a gentle tone.

Sangeeta slowly opened her eyes.

"Let's go," he said and led her outside the flight.

Her eyes fell immediately on the beautiful ocean and beach.

"This is a private resort," he said. "No one will disturb us. Even the employees working here would come only when you call for them."

Sangeeta nodded even though she slowly began to feel overwhelmed by everything. Private jets, private resorts and a business empire. It felt like a dream, too surreal. And she wasn't sure if she enjoyed the feeling much.

She somehow felt inadequate.

Her eyes fell on Vikram who was speaking softly to someone dressed in a uniform.

How did such a man fall in love with me? Does he even want me? Did he marry me because he felt obligated to?

She was reminded of Vishal's words from a while ago when he had told her that Vikram was shown hundreds of pictures of eligible brides. Now that Sangeeta knew how eligible those other women might have been, doubts began to creep in, and she became more nervous.

She jumped slightly when she heard Vikram's voice. "What do you want to have for dinner?" he asked as he led them inside the beach house.

Sangeeta's stomach felt queasy with nervousness and she couldn't think of eating anything. "I'm not hungry," she said. "I've had too much food in the last few days. I'll skip dinner."

Vikram watched her nervous face. "Take a relaxing bath," he said softly. "I'll order a simple meal. You can eat if you feel like it after your bath."

Nodding her head, she went towards her luggage. And then, grabbing a pair of night clothes, she ran into the bathroom. Even the bathroom made her nervous with the sheer size of it. It was much bigger than her bedroom in Srirampur.

Deciding to push away all of her, Sangeeta played around with the taps and sniffed a few bath salts until the huge sunken bathtub was filled with wonderful smelling, warm, sudsy water that was bubbling with the jets.

She stepped in and slowly sank inside until she was neck and shoulder-deep in the water.

She sighed in relief.

She was just about to drift off to sleep when she heard a knock on the door.

"Are you all right in there?" Vikram asked from outside.

"Yes! Give me a minute." She stood up and stepped out of the tub before hurriedly drying herself.

She put on her nightdress. Looking at herself in the mirror, she felt inadequate once again. The simple peach colored satin gown had felt appropriate when she had shopped for her honeymoon. But now, she wondered whether Vikram would find it cheap because he was probably used to being with women who wore expensive designer wear that were racier.

"Sangeeta?" Vikram called once again.

Breathing through her mouth, she stepped away from the mirror and slowly opened the door.

Vikram was standing near the large window that covered up most of the wall and overlooked the ocean.

He turned towards her when he heard the bathroom door shut. As soon as his eyes fell on her, he paused.

Oh God! He does think my lingerie is cheap.

With a slightly grim look, he came towards her and stood in front of her.

He cupped her cheek. "What's wrong?" he asked. "You seem upset and nervous."

"Nothing," she said quickly.

"Sangeeta," he said. "If it were just nervousness, I could've understood. But I don't understand why you seem upset."

She took a deep breath deciding to lay out the truth. Yes, she would come off as insecure, but she had to let him know how she felt. "It's just that... I know I'm not as attractive or appealing as the women you must be used to seeing with your lifestyle."

Disbelief flashed in his eyes.

But she continued. "You are from a different world, and I'm not—"

Before she could finish, he pulled her close and kissed the remaining words off.

He raised his head only when she was left gasping for breath and her heart was beating crazily in her chest. He swept her off the floor and carried her to his bed. When he laid her on it and settled on top of her, she couldn't speak because of the raw need she saw in his eyes.

"When I finally let you out of my bed... you, my love, will have no doubts about how much I need you and want you." His hands began to remove her clothes. "By the end of this night, you'll know how completely we belong with each other. Our different worlds be damned."

Soon, both of their clothes were gone. Sangeeta gasped as she absorbed the feel of their naked bodies pressed together. She could feel his heartbeat through his hard, muscled and hair-roughened wide chest. Her legs were nudged apart, and she felt every inch of his need lying against where her body throbbed in hunger.

"That is my body screaming for you," he growled.

He bent his head to kiss her again. And when the kisses got too heated, he moved lower to kiss her throat. Tingles and small tremors took over her body at the exploration.

He wasn't going slow. Even though he knew she was not very experienced, it was as if he knew and understood the need she had for him. And he also understood the need she had for him to want her.

He moved lower to kiss the tips of her breasts. He drew a rosy tip into his mouth and stroked the nipple with his tongue.

She gasped and clutched his head. When she thought, she couldn't bear the need anymore, he moved further lower. He kissed her quivering stomach before moving to where the source of her need originated.

She grabbed his hair. "Vikram!"

"Trust me," he said before kissing her in the most intimate part of her. She gasped, and she shuddered, and the feelings were beyond overwhelming. When she couldn't take it anymore, he moved up her body to kiss her lips.

And then, he reached down between them to guide himself inside her. He entered her, filling her. They both groaned at the moment of joining, his hardness enclosed against her softness, fusing their bodies completely.

Sangeeta held on to him, her hands moving over his flexing back while his hands held her hips. He pulled her close each time to receive his thrusts.

She shuddered in pleasure at each deep thrust. His mouth captured hers again in a long, deep kiss before raising his head and looking at her intently. "Never doubt my need and love for you," he said continuing to thrust.

"Never," she whispered through her kiss-swollen lips.

Soon, he began to move even faster. She clung to him until pleasure peaked and a rush of release ripped through her. Vaguely, she heard him groan as he joined her.

It took her a while to catch her breath and regain her senses. And then, with wonder filling her, she raised her hand and ran it along his damp, sweaty face.

He smiled and then turned his head to kiss her palm before leaning down and kissing her forehead which was equally sweaty as his.

"I love you," he said.

And then, he moved his head slightly lower and kissed her tenderly on her lips. But soon, his kisses began to turn deeper and hungry once again, filling her with a similar need.

She lost count of the number of times they made love that night.

Soon, it was dawn and the sky lit up beautifully outside.

"Sleep, my love," she heard him say as he tenderly smoothed her hair and pulled her close so she lay against him in a comfortable position.

She placed her hand on the center of his chest and closed her eyes to slip into a deep, content sleep with a smile on her face.

Sangeeta Saaho had no more doubts remaining as to whether or not the man she madly loved wanted and loved her in return.

CHAPTER FORTY-THREE

Three years later

"You do all realize that I am a doctor?" Sangeeta asked her family in exasperation.

She was seated in a large courtyard in her newly built house in Srirampur. They called it the Saaho house and it was right across the Gulati house.

Currently, Sangeeta was surrounded by her hovering family who was watching her anxiously.

"Ma, this is just Braxton Hicks," she told her anxious mother-in-law. "These are false contractions. I'm not about to deliver a baby prematurely in the second trimester."

"You should rest more often," a gruff masculine voice said. "Doesn't she work too hard?" Vishwanath Saaho asked his friend.

Suryaprakash Gulati nodded his agreement.

Sangeeta rolled her eyes and laughed. As if Grandpa would ever disagree with whatever his best friend said.

"Really, Grandfather," she said addressing Vishwanath Saaho. "You and Grandpa are always in the sun, overseeing so many things until the dusk. I am the one telling you both repeatedly that at your age, you should be resting more often."

"First ask your husband to stop traveling so often with a pregnant wife at home," Vishwanath Saaho advised. "Family is more important than work. We have enough."

"I was only away for a week in the last five months," a dry reply came from Vikram. "The rest of the time doesn't count because Sangeeta was with me during those trips."

"Well... a week is too much at this point. You should ask Vishal to oversee the North American operations, too."

Vikram was amused, especially when such statements came from a former workaholic.

"When is Vishu supposed to come to Srirampur, anyway?" Vinita Saaho asked.

Sangeeta looked at her watch. "Right about now."

Vinita looked excited. "Has Bhanu reached the location?" she asked.

"Yes, she did." Sangeeta was amused at the gleeful anticipation on her mother-in-law's face.

"Vinny!" Rajesh Saaho laughed. "You, my love, are way too scheming."

"Hah! As if each and every one of you weren't involved in some way or the other."

Rajesh Saaho smiled. "Well. Let's just hope things turn out the way they were planned."

***

Bhanu was nervous. She was seated in the driver's seat of a car waiting for quite a while.

"Deep breaths, Bhanu," she said aloud. "Deep breaths."

Until a while ago, her plan seemed like a great idea. She would wait at this place while posing as a uniformed chauffeur who was there to pick up Vishal. And instead of driving him to the Saaho house, Bhanu would take a detour where she would pull over and demand that Vishal listen to what she had to say.

But would Vishal listen to her?

Bhanu recalled all the times over the past three years she and Vishal had come across each other. There were only a handful of times that they saw each other during important family occasions. Each time Bhanu saw him, he completely ignored her. The first few times, she managed to speak a few words with him and apologized to him. But he only nodded politely, looking completely bored. So she gave up and decided not to broach the subject anymore thinking it would lead to awkwardness within their families.

Bhanu had felt deeply hurt by his continuing indifference, but it only made her more determined. She went from wanting to be a rich man's mistress to finishing a dual Master's Degree, one in Computers and the other in MBA. And now, she and some of her good friends were going to start a company right outside of Srirampur.

Higher education paired along with some amount of experience gave her the confidence to deal with the real world. If at the age of twenty-five, she was able to convince a major bank to offer loan and also convince a few well-known investors to invest in her start-up company, why couldn't she convince the man she loved to listen to her for a few minutes?

Yes. I'm an independent and confident woman. I will, and I can convince Vishu to listen to me.

But even with the pep talk, as soon as she heard a faint whirring sound, her stomach began to flutter once again in nervousness.

Oh God! Vishu is going to be here soon! He'll ignore me. He'll hate me. He might even— She pushed away her negative thoughts by taking in another deep breath.

The helicopter could have landed much closer to the Saaho and Gulati house, but since Sangeeta was pregnant, the pilot was told to land at a place much further away.

It was a ridiculous excuse, but it was made believable by the overprotective Gulati-Saaho family who didn't want any loud noises to affect the baby.

Bhanu continued to breathe through her mouth when the helicopter landed and the door opened.

She saw Tanuj getting down first. And later, he was followed by Vishal. Vishal gave instructions to Tanuj before walking towards the car.

Soon, he opened the backdoor of the car and got in. Bhanu was very thankful when he remained silent. His head was bent down while he typed something into his phone.

She started the car and drove them away.

There was silence in the car for the next thirty minutes until he spoke. "Why are you not heading to the Saaho house?" his crisp voice snapped.

"Because I want to talk to you."

Even though she had spoken in a soft voice, through the rearview mirror, she could see him stiffen as he recognized her voice.

"Stop the car," he ordered.

"I can't," she said. "We are in the middle of nowhere. You won't be able to find any other transportation."

"I don't care. Stop the car."

"I told you, I can't. Not when you are angry and possibly drunk. It's not safe to leave you on the side of the road."

Bhanu had spoken to Tanuj and asked him to stock up on alcohol during the helicopter ride. She wanted Vishal to be pliable and willing to listen to what she said. Tanuj had sounded amused, but had agreed to place an ice box filled with beer.

"I'm not drunk because I don't drink," he snapped. As soon as he let that fact slip, his face shut off once again.

Warmth and love expanded in Bhanu's heart listening to that information. It gave her the much-needed confidence to take her plan to its end. "Why?" she asked softly. "Why did you stop drinking?"

He ignored her question. "Stop the car, Bhanu," he ordered firmly instead.

Bhanu did as he ordered and pulled the car over. But instead of on the highway, she drove them to a spot where they often had gone three years ago while he was working as her driver. The place where they had made passionate love many times.

Vishal got out of the car and began walking away. He dialed a number on his phone and held it to his ear. "I'm sending you the coordinates," he told someone on the phone. "Get the helicopter back after refueling. I'm cutting short my stay."

Bhanu's heart sank. She hoped that Tanuj would delay his return or even not follow the order of his boss. But she knew Tanuj would have no choice.

Bhanu took longer and faster steps to catch up and grabbed Vishal's hand to stop him. She felt him stiffen at her touch, but he didn't pull his hand away.

"Please, Vishal. I want you to listen," she said urgently.

Vishal turned to look at her and glowered at her. "You are way out of line with such behavior," he growled.

She smiled tentatively at him. "I-I know. But didn't you once say that you liked aggressive and stubborn brats?" she reminded.

He was silent and continued to glower.

"I've said this before and I'm saying it now once again. I'm sorry, Vishu," she said. "I love my grandfather. He is all I have apart from Sangeeta. And I—"

His eyes flared in a fury before he cut her off. "You know damn well I wasn't angry because I thought you chose your grandfather over me. I was angry because you didn't even put up a bloody fight. You were willing to marry someone else and sacrifice our love just so you didn't disappoint your grandfather."

Bhanu knew he was right. She also knew that he warranted his anger and grudge for this long because of that fact. "I'm sorry," she said softly. "There are no excuses, except for the fact that I was scared. Even when I fell in love with you when you pretended to be my driver, I was scared for having such strong feelings for someone I barely knew. And when I knew your real identity, I just felt too overwhelmed. I questioned myself whether someone like you could really feel that way about someone like me."

"Someone like me?" he asked in a dangerous tone.

"You were known for your playboy ways, and I saw the pictures of you with many high-profile beautiful women you dated—"

"If you didn't trust my love then, why trust me now?" he demanded.

"Because I'm not the same immature or insecure girl from three years ago." She smiled tentatively again before adding, "Hopefully."

When he didn't return the smile, she continued to pour her heart out. "I wasn't mature or level-headed like Sangeeta who knew what she wanted out of her life. I had ambitions, too, but I didn't seek them out. Instead, I pursued a stupid idea to be a rich man's mistress because of my hurt ego. But I don't regret it because it got me you. And now that I have achieved a part of my dream, I want to pursue the most important part. You."

Vishal watched her with an expressionless look.

"Say something," she whispered.

He pulled his hand away from her grip, making her stomach sink. But the next moment, he grabbed her hand and jerked her to him until her body crashed against his. He held the back of her head, and bent down closer, until barely an inch was left between their mouths.

Her breath came out in soft pants as she stared into his stormy eyes. Before she embarrassed herself by begging him to kiss her, he kissed her.

Her eyes shut and her knees buckled at the sheer intensity and the memories that flooded her mind.

She kissed him back and she vaguely felt him picking her up and carrying her somewhere. When he lowered her, even after three long years, the feel of the slightly soft yet rough hay felt familiar on her back.

He continued to kiss her even as he began to remove her clothes. With frantic hands, she reached out to him and began to unbutton his shirt.

He wasn't careful. She felt a few buttons from her shirt fly as he more or less ripped it apart. She did the same with his shirt and soon, she felt his bare skin on top of hers.

She widened her legs even before he could push them apart. Within moments, he joined them together. She gasped when pain and pleasure warred together. But soon, she was completely lost in a world of passion. She was as desperate for him as he was for her to join their bodies along with their hearts and souls.

But it was over too soon. Three years of separation had made them too impatient and hungry for one another.

Later, when they could slowly catch their breaths, he rolled away and pulled her on top of him, until she lay on his chest. She sighed in content, listening to his thumping heartbeat, and feeling like she was finally home. She lay in the arms of the man she loved.

But she knew there were too many things that still needed to be said and cleared and resolved. "Vishu—" She began to speak, but broke off frowning when she heard a faint whirring sound.

Tanuj was bringing back the chopper.

"Oh my God!" Bhanu tried to roll away but Vishal didn't let her go.

"Vishu, let me go!" she said frantically. "Tanuj is bringing back the helicopter and will see us!"

Slowly and reluctantly, Vishal loosened the hold on her.

Even as she felt the loss of his heat and touch, she stood up and scrambled for her clothes. She slipped into her underclothes and tried to button up her wrinkled shirt with many of its buttons missing.

Her eyes fell on Vishal who hadn't bothered to move from the spot and was watching her lazily. His eyes were slowly tracking her every moment and familiarizing himself with her body.

Even though her body was sore and he had just finished making hard, furious and energetic love to her, her body began to tingle. But the sound of the chopper snapped her from the spell.

"Vishu! Put on your clothes! Or Tanuj will know what we were up to."

Vishal just grinned slowly, causing her stomach to flip crazily. She was reminded of the old Vishal, her cocky and arrogant driver, the man she had fallen in love with.

"Flash news, Princess," he drawled. "Not just Tanuj, everyone already knows what we are up to. And the fact that we'll be disappearing together for the next few days, it'll make it even more obvious."

"We can't just disappear!"

"Oh, we can," he said with confidence. "You think a quick romp in the hay would satisfy my three years of self-imposed abstinence and hunger for you?"

He leaped up naked and dragged her close. "Three years," he growled. "I've waited for three long, bloody years."

Her heart began to thud inside her chest as happiness and excitement fought to dominate each other.

He looked into her eyes and she saw raw emotion swirling within. "You have no idea how many bloody times Vikram and the rest of our family had to stop me from going after you, and dragging you back to me." His nostrils flared. "I have never hated the words *'time'* and *'space'* as much as I did in the last three years when our family used it to reason with me of why I needed to stay away from you."

"And you listened?" she whispered.

"Yes. Because they were speaking the truth," he said grudgingly. "You were right in having doubts about us in the past. Our love hit us both way too fast. You were only twenty-one and had never seen the outside world. I was with way too many women and never had a serious relationship with anyone before. But this long break only proved what I always knew. Our love can withstand the test of any amount of time and distance."

Even though a major part of her was thrilled and excited they were getting back together, a part of her was puzzled by the entire line of conversation.

"If you felt that way, then why were you so angry with me when I came to pick you up today?" she asked.

"Because," he growled. "The moment you graduated, you were supposed to run back into my arms. You made me wait six more bloody months!"

She shook her head. "I'm sorry. I didn't know how to get to you the last few months," she explained. "You had always avoided coming to family reunions when I was around. I had to plan this trip in an underhanded way. Geeta kept it a secret from everyone even though she knew. I even kept badgering Geeta over the last three years asking her if you were seeing any women. She'll be quite relieved that I'll no longer ask her to be my spy."

"There was no one," he clarified. "Because there wasn't a single day when my mind wasn't filled with thoughts of you or us together. Even during your absence, you were a huge pain in my butt, Princess."

She laughed. "I'm so glad."

"But you are going to pay me back. I'm keeping you captive." He slowly grinned. "And letting you out of my bed only for some light wedding shopping."

"I—" She broke off and frowned in confusion. "Wait. Wedding shopping?"

He pulled her close and kissed her, making her heart beat crazily again. "When we get back, our family will be waiting for us. And hopefully, you'll agree to marry me in two weeks." He gave her the details of the exact date including the time.

Bhanu held her breath, and she stared at him, shocked.

It took a few moments, but even through the happy haze, her brain worked overtime and she figured it out. The sound of the helicopter remained faint, making it obvious that Tanuj was instructed not to arrive at the exact location. It reeked of a predetermined plan.

"You planned this!" she accused. "I thought I more or less kidnapped you and brought you here to beg for your forgiveness and ask you to take me back. But all the while you knew, and this was *your* plan to get me here! **This is your damn proposal**!" She more or less shouted the last part.

He grinned. "Yes. This is my proposal. Sangeeta and Mum helped me by planting ideas into your head."

Another wiggling doubt crept into her head. She sucked in a breath. "When did you tell our family about wanting to marry me?"

"Three years ago," he replied, confirming her doubt. "I took our grandfathers' approvals three years ago the day Vikram proposed to Sangeeta. I told them that we'd be getting married soon after you finish your Master's Degree. A month ago, I gave them that the exact date and told them I'm going to propose to you today."

Bhanu stared at him for a few shock-filled moments. And then, she leaped on him with a furious look.

"I'm going to kiiiiilllll you!" she shouted.

She wanted to pound him to a pulp for putting her through hell these last three years thinking that she had lost the love of her life and that the man she desperately loved didn't even care for her the least bit.

But before she could pound him on his chest, he caught her and wrapped his arms around her, and kissed her hard, robbing her of her breath.

When he finally let her mouth go, they were both panting.

She glared at him. "You are... such a... high-handed... arrogant... ass!" she shouted. She sucked in more breaths before continuing with more threats. "You so deserve to have me as your wife. I'm going to get back at you in so many ways for putting me through this!"

The infuriating man just grinned. "Can't wait, Princess."

With his dimples flashing, he again looked every inch the high-handed sexy, arrogant devil she had fallen head over heels in love with. And so, her anger and outrage disappeared as quickly as they arose.

There was a flash of possessiveness in his eyes and he pulled her close. "Say it!" he demanded.

She wanted to torture him by delaying her answer, but the vulnerability she saw in his eyes while his face remained cocky and arrogant made her give in.

"I love you, you arrogant devil!" she snapped. "And yes, I'll marry you."

He let out a joyful laugh at her reply and hugged her tightly. "I love you so damn much, Princess. And I can't wait to spend the rest of our lives together."

The End.

Author's Note

Thank you for reading *The Promise*. It was quite a different experience for me to write two romantic yet very different love stories in one single book. Vikram and Sangeeta's love, although intense, was sweet and understated while Vishal and Bhanu's was hot, raw and passionate. Amidst the two younger couple's love stories was the underlying older couple's love triangle and friendship which drove the main plot.

In my mind, Vikram and Vishal are the quintessential heroes with Vikram being the silent, brooding kind and Vishal being the cocky, bad-boy type. Sangeeta and Bhanu's back story and their characteristics were inspired by Jane Austen's *Sense and Sensibility*. Sangeeta is the sweet, sensible and gentle sister while Bhanu is the fiery, impulsive and passionate one.

I loved all four of them with their own unique quirks, flaws and strengths. I hope you loved them too! :)

Thank You!

MV Kasi

Email: manyavkasi@gmail.com

FB/Instagram: @mvkasi

M. V. Kasi's Book List

WICKED TRAP
WICKED LIES
WICKED DECEPTION
WILD IN LOVE
CRASH IN LOVE
DEVIL'S LOVE
DEVIL'S DESIRE
DEVIL'S KISS
UNTIL YOU
ACCIDENTAL HUSBAND
THE PROMISE
THAT SAME OLD LOVE
THE HOLIDAY AFFAIR
MISSION SUPERSTAR
UNTIL FOREVER
BOUND BY HATRED
THE CAPTIVE
SOULLESS
RUTHLESS
BREATHLESS

Short Stories (20-Minute Reads)

HIS CAPTIVE BRIDE
RECKLESS LOVE
THE ROYAL WEDDING
THE PROPOSAL
BOUND BY FOREVER
BILLIONAIRE ESCORT